FINTA

Gavan leaned closer; Jamie could smell incense and tobacco and leather.

'Now,' Morgant said, 'are you ready?'

Jamie nodded, but the question was not for him. Unravelling itself across the page like a black thread, the answer wrote itself swiftly:

I am ready.

The dim light from the oil lamp flickered; their three huge hunchbacked shadows rippled on the ceiling. Jamie let his breath out slowly. 'It's amazing!'

'Quite.' Morgant gave him a small smile. 'But I think you will be seeing stranger things soon. Now, you must do the asking. The Book will only answer you, or rather, will only give you the information we need. Here is a list of questions I have prepared.'

Jamie looked at them, then at the Book. 'Where is the Prisoner?' he said.

The Prisoner is in Fintan's Tower.

Catherine Fisher
—
FINTAN'S TOWER

RED FOX

A Red Fox Book

Published by Random House Children's Books
20 Vauxhall Bridge Road, London SW1V 2SA

A division of Random House UK Ltd
London Melbourne Sydney Auckland
Johannesburg and agencies throughout the world

First published by The Bodley Head Children's Books 1991

Red Fox edition 1992

Printed and bound in Great Britain by
Cox & Wyman Ltd, Reading, Berkshire

ISBN 0 09 993520 1

Contents

HERE

1. The Green Baize Door   3
2. Book Fair   9
3. The Man in the Lane   15
4. Directions   21
5. In the Barn   27
6. Cai   35
7. Eclipse   42

THERE

8. The Black Wood   53
9. Down the Cliff   62
10. Theft   70
11. The Man from Yesterday   77
12. Fortress of Frustration   85
13. Fortress of Carousal   92
14. The Prison of Gweir   97
15. The Wisdom of the Cauldron   106
16. Return to Logria   114

Author's Note   120

To Toady and Moly

The author gratefully acknowledgés the financial assistance of the Welsh Arts Council during the writing of this book.

HERE

. . . yg kynneir or peir pan leferit
Oanadyl naw morwyn gochyneuit . . .

. . . my first utterance, it is from the Cauldron that it was
spoken.
By the breath of nine maidens it was kindled . . .

The Spoils of Annwn

1
The Green Baize Door

'We're closing,' the librarian said, looking up at the clock, 'in exactly three minutes. Books or not.'

'All right.' *Keep your hair on.* Jamie tipped out a promising title from the shelf, then pulled a face and pushed it back. Why didn't they ever get anything new? Every week it was the same old tatty plastic jackets full of boring-looking kids with anoraks and torches – no ghosts, or astronomy, or crusaders. What he wanted was a book that was different.

'Two minutes,' the librarian snapped.

Junior Fiction was in a dim corner by the window that looked down into Grape Lane. Rain ran down the glass and streaked the dirt. Jamie pulled up a stool and glared at the rows of books. Come on, there must be something. It was three weeks since he'd last found a new one, and that had been about a tribe of intelligent rats who took over the London Underground. Well, they might have been intelligent, but whoever wrote the book wasn't . . .

The street door flew open; a big, red-haired man splashed in, his mac glossy with rain. He marched straight up to the desk.

'We're closed,' the librarian said. She didn't even look up.

The man wore a tartan scarf that covered half his face. His eyes were small and rather bloodshot, with no expression. Deliberately he reached out, took the

Biro from her fingers and snapped it into two pieces, his eyes never leaving her face. Then he flung the pieces into the metal bin one by one; two loud explosions.

Jamie held his breath.

Arms folded, the librarian surveyed the stranger. 'There's a button under this desk,' she said firmly, 'which rings a bell in the police station.'

The big man put both hands down flat and leaned over. 'Don't waste my time, woman,' he growled. 'I'm here to see the Name in the Book.'

To Jamie's surprise the librarian blinked. She took off her glasses and her eyes were green as glass and glinted in the shadows. 'Oh, I see,' she said slowly. 'I see. Well, you should have said before, shouldn't you. It's over there, through the green baize door.'

The man smiled, rather unpleasantly, and picked up his streaming umbrella. He crossed the library and pushed through a small door that Jamie had not noticed before; it was in a dark corner behind some shelves. The door swished shut, silently. A chill draught swept across the room, ruffling the pages of some books.

Jamie turned back to the tatty jackets. The librarian found another pen and carried on writing; the clock ticked on towards half-past four; rain tapped and rattled on the window. Listlessly, Jamie flicked the pages of a manual on hang-gliding. Then he froze.

'I wonder, my dear, if you could help me. They are saying that the Name is in the Book.'

This time it was an oldish man in a tweed coat. He was short, and had a small, clever face with a stubbly grey beard. His scarf, tucked in out of the rain, poked from between his second and third buttons, and he carried a large canvas bag.

4

The librarian shrugged. 'Another one. You're late.'

'Oh, I've come a long, long way. I gather from your remark that I am not the first.'

'No. Now hurry up please, we're closing. Over there through the baize door.'

Intrigued, Jamie watched the old man walk eagerly between the shelves and open the door. It swung silently behind him.

Far off, the church clock began to chime the half-hour; water gurgled down the drainpipes outside. The librarian hummed to herself, licking a paper label. Jamie watched the door. Neither of the men had come back. What book were they looking for? They couldn't both borrow it. And what was all this about a name?

Then, on the last stroke of the clock, the door from the street was hurled wide, and a tall, fair-haired man burst in through a squall of rain. He flung himself at the desk; Jamie had a sudden shiver of anticipation.

'Listen!' said the man breathlessly. 'I've got to see the Name in the Book!'

A gasp came from Junior Fiction. The man spun round like a flash, but no one was there.

The librarian waved the sticky label. 'Green door. Better hurry.'

The stranger raced across the room and disappeared with a slam and a draught.

Right! Jamie thought. He stood up, pocketed his tickets and walked over to the desk. The librarian glared.

'Are you still here? Out! We're closed.'

Jamie rolled his hands into fists in his pockets.

'I hear,' he said, 'that the Name is in the Book.'

'What?'

'The Name is in the Book.'

She wrinkled her eyes up and pushed out her bottom lip. For a moment Jamie felt almost afraid. Something cold nudged against his heart. But all she said was: 'If you say so. The green door, in the corner.'

His heart thumping, Jamie followed the trail of wet footprints across the floor. When he reached the door he looked back. The librarian was looking after him with a particularly unpleasant smile.

'Good luck,' she said. 'You'll need it.'

On the other side of the door was a dark, damp landing, so damp his breath made a cloud in the air. To his left, a narrow wooden stair ran down into darkness, and a tiny window in the wall let in some bleared light.

He padded softly down. The steps were slimy, and they sounded hollow under his boots. At the bottom was a short passage, with puddles on the floor. Down here the walls were stone, icy cold under his fingers. Ahead of him was an archway, and through that he could see a room, empty, except for books. Books on shelves, books stacked in toppling towers on the floor, books fallen from broken chairs; all of them covered with years of dust and grime and webs.

His fingers found a light switch, and after a moment's silence, he pressed it. Weak light gleamed from a bulb in the ceiling.

No one else was in the room, but a trail of footprints led past a big wooden table to a door in the opposite wall. Jamie crossed the room and unlatched it. Rain splashed his face. He was looking out into the alley at the back of the building; putting his head out he could see an old iron lamppost halfway down in the darkness, dropping a pool of light on to the wet cobbles.

Tiny arrows of rain flashed across it. He looked the other way. No one. It was silent, just a wet crack between the houses.

So why had they come, those three strangers? Stepping back into the basement he closed the door and went over to the table.

On it was a book. One book, by itself; smaller than most of the others in the room. The cobwebs had been wiped off it. The cover was of plain black leather, with no title, just a single tiny picture in the centre. He put a finger on it; it was hard and shiny as if made of glass, or enamel. It showed a bright blue sky and a landscape of tiny fields, hedges and hills, all in deep lustrous greens. Far off on the horizon was something grey, a dark tinge in the glass.

Jamie opened the book. Inside, on the first clean white page, a name was beautifully written in italics:

James Michael Meyrick

He stood there, stiff with surprise, reading those three familiar words over and over. Who had written his name? Who knew that he would come down here? After all, he hadn't known himself until that sudden daft idea upstairs.

Then the truth struck him like a sharp pain. The Name in the Book. It was his.

After a moment he thumbed through the rest of the pages. They were blank. For a second he thought he had glimpsed something, and turned back, but no, each page was white and empty. It was a thin book, only about fifty pages in all. Carefully, he laid it down. It fitted into the dust, in a square of clean desk. That meant . . . well, it must mean it had lain there undisturbed for years – until now. Those three had opened

it, and read his name. He put out a finger and gingerly
flicked the cover open again, half hoping it might have
gone away. But there it was. And underneath, in the
same spiky letters:

Take me home.

Suddenly, Jamie snapped the Book shut, stuffed it
into his inside pocket and unlatched the back door.
In the alley rain gurgled in culverts and drains; the sky
was dim between the overhanging houses. He stepped
outside and slammed the door. Pulling on his hood,
he shoved his hands deep in his pockets and splashed
through the pool of light from the lamppost, and away
into the dark.

2
Book Fair

'What's this?' Jennie tapped the Book with her pencil. 'Don't tell me they've actually got something new!'

'It's not a library book.' He looked over but it was already too late. She had opened it and was flicking through the pages.

'Mmm. I see what you mean. Nice pictures though.'

'Pictures?' Jamie threw down the wool he had been tangling round the kitten and jumped up. 'What pictures?'

He took the book from her and looked through the pages, carefully. They were empty, just as they had been yesterday and this morning; even those three words he thought he had seen were gone. There was just his name, familiar and faintly mocking.

He turned his head. 'Which picture did you like best?' He tried to keep the eagerness out of his voice. Jennie shrugged over her homework. 'Oh, I don't know. The one at the back, I suppose – the tower with the figure on top.'

'What figure?'

'Well, look for yourself, Jamie. A gargoyle thing, a sentinel. And that light in the top window.' She became immersed in the fate of Sir Thomas More.

Jamie sat himself down on the step and leaned against the open door. In front of him the garden rolled smoothly downhill; out of sight in the willows at the bottom he could hear the Caston Brook running down to the bridge. The grass was thick with leaves; wet blackened masses of them lay clotting in the kitchen drain, and in heaps against the wall. Rooks clung and squawked in the elms.

It was all wrong. Who had written the words, and how had they vanished again? He thought vaguely of invisible inks, heat treatment, mysterious cosmic rays.

He got up and wandered down to the brook. It was narrow here, and the trees met overhead and dropped their leaves into the fast brown water. There was a hole in the bank that he thought might be a rat's. The kitten came after him, dragging a trail of wool through the grass.

He sat on the bank and examined the picture on the Book's cover, for at least the tenth time. What was that dim mark on the furthest hill? It seemed nearer than before. It looked like a house, or . . . Struck by an idea, he ran into the house and came back with a magnifying glass. Lying full length in the willow leaves, he held it carefully over the tiny enamel.

It was a castle. Small, and greeny-grey, but complete. How could anyone paint that small? Even the battlements were perfect, and that faint point of light shining from the high window. Then, with a jerk, he gripped the magnifying glass tight. The light had gone out! He looked again, but the window was dark.

'Jamie!' His mother stood over him. 'Get up off the grass, will you. This just came.' She threw down a small brown envelope, which was addressed to him in delicate spidery writing. 'I'm going into the market now. Want anything?'

He shook his head absently and opened the envelope. A card fell out.

'It's about a book sale,' he said, puzzled. 'Who'd send it to me?'

'Well, you read books, don't you?' His mother came and took it. 'That's today. You can walk down with me, if you like. You might find some cheap paperbacks, or something.'

While Mrs Meyrick searched for her purse, Jamie ran upstairs. He wanted to put the Book away, but as he moved he thought he saw something inside and fumbled hurriedly with the pages. There! The words were written on a page near the centre, in the same writing:

I would be careful if I were you.

It was incredible. Who was writing it – it couldn't write itself, could it? He fingered the back of the page – no magnetic strips. Nothing in the paper. Nothing. 'Careful of what?' he whispered. But the rest of the pages were blank.

With a kind of fear he locked the Book in the cupboard at the side of his bed, then hid the key in its usual place in the hole in his mattress, under the pillow. There was a place for it there, but he had to be careful or it slipped down among the springs and was difficult to get out again.

The warning – if it was one – stuck in his head as he ran downstairs and saw his mother waiting in the porch. Was it possible the Book meant it for him? He shook his head. The thing couldn't be alive. It was just paper. His mother was waiting in the porch. 'Come on,' she said. 'Before the coaches start.'

Like most of the houses in Caston, theirs was an old building, its front black-timbered, with white plaster making strange uneven squares and crosses. The porch was carved with grotesque little goblins that squatted and leered at callers – the milkman always said theirs were the ugliest in town, and that was saying a lot.

Caston High Street turned and twisted for half a mile; its houses were humped and huddled and squeezed together, their upper storeys jutting out over the cobbles and the narrow pavement that sometimes disappeared altogether. Cars roared along the one-way system; as Jamie passed the post office a coachload of tourists swirled dust into his eyes.

At the Market Hall his mother stopped. 'Don't spend too much, and don't buy rubbish. We've enough old books in the house as it is.'

'All right.' He watched her march through the doors into the dim hall with its stalls of bananas and leatherwork and home-made cakes and love spoons. His mother never walked anywhere; she marched, and dragged you with her.

Now he could dawdle. Already the tourist shops by the church were putting out their racks of postcards and tea towels with leeks on, and the Welsh words for bread and cheese, and already one or two early visitors were photographing the almshouses with their leaning doorways. He took the short cut through Pike's Alley, then through Quiver Street and Llywelyn's Street, and came out by the bridge, where the Caston Brook swirled underneath with fish in its green hair. If you put in a cork at the garden at home,

12

it took two and a half minutes to get here; he and Jennie had tried it more than once with a stopwatch.

The Tithe Barn was over the bridge and up a short muddy lane. It was probably the oldest building in the town, but somehow or other the visitors always seemed to miss it. It stood remote and quiet in its weeds; jackdaws stole its thatch, and a barn owl nested in a hole in the eaves.

He pushed open the heavy door and went in. It was usually silent and empty, but this morning there were tables and bookshelves all around. The noise of talk echoed in the roof.

'Ten pence!' demanded a small girl behind the door, and when he gave it to her she handed him a pink ticket. 'Thank you.'

Each stall was jammed with books, most of them old and musty. After a while Jamie realized that most of them were too expensive for him, but there were one or two that he wished he could afford. The sweet, old-fashioned smell of them hung in the air; he began to enjoy rummaging in the dusty boxes and hearing the talk of folios and first editions.

It was at the stall in the corner, while he was looking at a picture of Saturn in an astronomy book priced two pounds, that he sensed someone watching him. He peered over the top of the page.

An old man sat on a stool, eating a sandwich. Their eyes met.

'Like it?' the man asked.

Jamie nodded. 'Bit expensive though.'

The man took another bite. He wore a pullover with a hole in the sleeve and black mittens with no fingers. His face was small and brown, with a short grey beard.

'Interested in books, are you?'

'Depends what they're about.' Jamie put the book back. Then he said, 'Weren't you in the library yesterday?'

The old man smiled. 'Ah, so you know about that. And you should, shouldn't you? It's your name that's in the Book.'

Despite all the noise and chatter around him, Jamie felt uneasy. Bewilderment with the whole thing bubbled up in him. 'Listen,' he said, 'can you explain to me about that Book? It's driving me mad. It has things written in it sometimes, and then, at other times . . .'

The old man nodded. 'Ah yes. I know all about it. The Book, you see, is your companion. It tells you the way, and the dangers.'

'The way to where?'

'Other worlds. Have you got it with you?'

The sudden question took Jamie off guard. 'Now? No, I haven't.'

'That's a pity.' The man fingered his stubbly beard. His eyes were bright, like beads. He pulled a card from his pocket. 'Look, my name is Morgant. Come and see me, at this house, tonight. We can tell you what you want to know.'

He turned to a customer who was holding a five-pound note, and began to count change out of the apron round his waist. 'Don't forget. Come tonight. Once the Name comes, there is little time to lose. We only have until the eclipse to get ready.'

'For what?' Jamie asked, bewildered.

'To rescue the Prisoner.'

3

The Man in the Lane

Jamie walked up the High Street with the Book in a plastic bag under his arm. It was half-past seven, and raining again; the goblin gargoyles over the houses were spouting mouthfuls of water down gutters and drains. Low grey cloud pressed on the town. At the corner a grinning wooden imp spat splashes on to his neck.

The High Street was well-lit, but Hanging Dog Lane was always black. It was an inky slot in the wall of houses, as if one of them had shuffled aside and left this thin, damp, evil-smelling gap. It led down to a labyrinth of alleys, back doorways, steps up and steps down, and blank walls with dingy windows no one looked through.

Jamie stopped at the corner. He distrusted this lane, the smell of it and the damp; it reminded him of thieves and cut-throats and a story he had once read of a creature that flopped down on travellers in the dark. His fingers touched the old man's stiff blue card.

> THE WATCH-HOUSE
> HANGING DOG LANE
> CASTON
> GWENT

Glancing once at the bats that flickered over the house-tops, he stepped in.

The cobbles were wet, and slippery. The alley was

so narrow he could easily put his hands on both side walls, and once out of the lights from the street he felt his way forward cautiously. No wonder it was an unpleasant place. The gallows had been down here somewhere, where they had hanged pickpockets and horse-thieves – and even a dog, so the story went, for stealing meat. Owen Hadley in school said the dog walked, even said he'd seen it. Black and velvety, with eyes like lamps; it slithered past your legs or padded after you without a sound.

Jamie stopped; his footsteps died into silence. Silence settled like dust on ledges and slates and sills. No padding. Well, after all, he thought, Owen Hadley had the biggest mouth in the school. And you'd never catch him down here at night.

Looking up, he saw that the stars were coming out, glittering in the ragged clouds. The dark houses leaned above him as if they had their heads together, gossiping.

Something made him turn and look back up the alley; there in the entrance, framed against the light, a man was standing. He was thin and tall, and he was looking down into the darkness of the lane, with his head slightly tilted, as if he was listening.

Jamie held the Book tight. Noiselessly he slid against the wall, not wanting to be seen.

The man waited, then stepped forward. His shadow grew huge in the rectangle of light, but as he came deeper into the alley the darkness swallowed him up; he became just a glimmer in the blackness.

'Jamie?'

Jamie jumped; the soft voice had run along the wall, echoing in pipes and gutters.

'I know you're here, Jamie. I saw you come in.'

16

The footsteps were quiet, but nearer. Frozen, Jamie stared into the shadows.

'I won't hurt you.'

He was close! Jamie's heart thudded; he began to edge away, silently sliding his feet over the slippery stones. A drain-pipe swung as he touched it, and clanged against its rusty bracket. At once a cold hand came out of the darkness and grabbed him.

'Listen,' the voice said. 'I want to talk to you.'

Jamie struggled and squirmed in panic. 'Let go of me!' he yelled, and the Book slid out from under his arm and they both lurched at it. Rain began to fall in large heavy drops.

Suddenly Jamie shoved the stranger backwards so that he crashed into the wet wall. Before he could get up, Jamie grabbed the Book and ran, sprinting up the alley with the rain in his face.

The lane twisted sharply; in the dark he ran into a wall, jumped down some steps and darted into a tiny courtyard full of dustbins. One dim lamp hung on the wall, lighting a ragged cinema poster. Jamie raced over to a doorway, threw himself in against the wood and listened. At first he could only hear his breathing and his heart thumping; then, in the stillness, a limp and shuffle in the lane. Footsteps came down the steps and paused; he could see a shadow stretched out in the lamplight.

'Listen, you little wretch,' snarled the voice. 'If I have to come and find you, you'll be sorry!'

There he was, standing in the lamplight, one hand on the wet wall. For the first time Jamie saw him clearly: a very tall man, with hair of a strange shining gold; dark angry eyes and a nose hooked like an eagle's beak. It was the third man from the library.

Puzzled, he was about to move when he felt sudden

17

emptiness behind him. A small cool hand slid round and clasped itself over his mouth.

'Not a sound,' the old man whispered, 'or he'll hear. Inside, quickly.' Jamie was drawn back into the dark, and saw the door close. The old man bent down and slid the bolts across. 'Did he see where you went?'

'No. At least, I don't think so. Listen . . .'

But the old man's hand tugged his sleeve. 'Not here. Upstairs.'

The stairs were wooden and twisted round on themselves, and creaked underfoot. Morgant led the way; they climbed up past two landings, both dusty and carpetless, and still up. Breathless, Jamie heard the old man puffing. 'Nearly there . . . it's the watchtower.' As he spoke he pushed open the door at the top and Jamie followed him into the room.

It was small, and octagonal; in each wall was a window of thick leaded glass, tinted blue and red and green. In the middle of the floor stood a circular table stained with rings and scorchmarks, and sitting with one arm sprawled across it, eating a large greasy hamburger, was the big red-haired man from the library. Number one and number two. So they're all in it, Jamie thought.

'Ah.' The red man swallowed a mouthful of bread. 'He's come! Good!' He grinned, nastily, and Jamie remembered how he had broken the librarian's pen.

'Sit here.' Morgant dusted a chair with a red handkerchief. 'Gavan, this room of ours is a piggery.'

The big man snorted. 'Has he got the Book, though?'

'He has. Now, Jamie, this is . . . Mr Gavan. Thank you for coming here – it must have been difficult.'

Jamie perched on the chair. 'Well, I wanted to find out about my name.'

18

'Ah yes.' Morgant put his elbows on the table and joined his fingertips together. 'But first, I'm a little worried. Who was your friend outside, the one who was chasing you?'

'I don't know. Isn't he with you?'

'With us!'

Jamie shrugged. 'Well, I just assumed the three of you were together. He came into the library after you . . .'

'*What!*' Gavan almost choked.

'Quiet,' Morgant snapped. 'Jamie, listen, this is vital. You mean there was a *third* man?'

'Yes.'

'And he looked at the Book?'

'I suppose so. He went down there. And outside, he knew my name.'

Gavan took a swig of beer from a mug. 'He's lying! There couldn't have been!'

Morgant glared at him. 'Will you save your breath to eat!' He turned back to Jamie. 'What does he look like?' He waggled his two joined fingers. 'Exactly, mind.'

'Very tall. Blond hair, dark eyes – brown, I think.' Jamie watched them both curiously. 'His face is narrow, with a hook nose like a hawk. He's younger than you, with a black coat . . .'

'Damn!' Gavan pounded the table so hard that Jamie jumped. 'It's that hellcat Cai! The worst of them!'

He stormed over to the window and glared down.

Morgant shook his head. He did not seem as surprised, Jamie thought. 'This is a serious problem,' he explained. 'We know this man, we've had dealings with him before. He is very dangerous, and quite unpredictable. His name is Cai. He wouldn't stop at bloodshed. If he'd got his hands on you out there . . .' Again, he shook his head.

Jamie thought of the angry face in the lamplight.

'I really had no idea,' Morgant went on, 'that anyone else had seen the Book after us.'

Jamie fiddled with the corner of the bag. 'Yes, but I don't get it. If he wanted the Book . . .'

'He could have taken it from the library? Yes, but you see, Jamie, your name is in it. The Book is useless without you; he wants you as well. The time is coming when the way between the worlds will be open; it will be easy to pass through. When this is so, the Book reappears and it bears a name. That person is the Book's Keeper for that time. But look' – he held up a hand to ward off Jamie's questions – 'why should I waste my old voice, mm? We'll let someone else explain. Gavan, the light, please.'

The big man jerked the curtains across and brought an oil lamp to the table, shoving the dirty plates aside. Shadows leapt and scurried over the ceiling. Morgant drew the Book from its bag, reverently, and placed it on a stand. He opened it at a clean white page. On a small saucer nearby he placed a pinch of grey powder from a gold box, and dropped a match into it. With a puff the powder ignited; it flared harshly. Gavan leaned closer; Jamie could smell incense and tobacco and leather.

'Now,' Morgant said, 'are you ready?'

Jamie nodded, but the question was not for him. Unravelling itself across the page like a black thread, the answer wrote itself swiftly:

I am ready.

4
Directions

The dim light from the oil lamp flickered; their three huge hunchbacked shadows rippled on the ceiling. Jamie let his breath out slowly. 'It's amazing!'

'Quite.' Morgant gave him a small smile. 'But I think you will be seeing stranger things soon. Now, you must do the asking. The Book will only answer you, or rather, will only give you the information we need. Here is a list of questions I have prepared.'

Jamie looked at them, then at the Book. 'Where is the Prisoner?' he said.

The Prisoner is in Fintan's Tower.

It wrote itself quickly, each letter beautifully formed.

'Good,' Morgant chuckled. 'But we knew that. The problem is, the Tower is never in the same place twice. Ask it how we get in.'

'Yes, but who's this prisoner?'

'I'll explain all that later. Come on.'

Jamie hesitated. He had half a mind to argue, but Gavan gripped his shoulder. 'Ask it!'

Ruffled, Jamie shook him off. 'All right! Keep your hands to yourself!' He turned back to the page. 'They want to know how to get to this place.'

The Book did not answer at once. Then it wrote:

The way to the Summer Country is long and perilous.

*Between the stones on the Harper's Beacon there is a
door. It will be open when the sun's eye closes on the day
of Samain. But take care! Few return from that country.*

'Excellent.' Morgant seemed to take no notice of the
warning. 'That part will be easy. And once we are in
that country?'

But the Book, when Jamie asked it, was keeping
some of its secrets.

I cannot yet say.

Gavan scowled. 'Make it say!' His fingernails, cracked
and dirty, drummed on the table.

'That would be foolish. We have plenty of time.'
Morgant seemed highly satisfied; he leaned back in
his chair and said, 'Now, Jamie, you say you have
questions of your own. Ask away.'

Surprised, Jamie turned to the Book. 'What I want
to know is . . . well, who is this prisoner?'

His name is Gweir, the Book wrote promptly.

'Great. And why is he locked up in this place?'

There was a pause; this time the writing unrolled
more thoughtfully:

*The reason is lost in time. Some say that at three days old
he was stolen from between his mother and the wall. The
truth may be that he went with the Emperor to steal the
Cauldron, and was captured.*

'You're a mine of information,' Jamie remarked.
'*What* cauldron?'

Even the King of Annwn's Cauldron. Dark blue it is:

22

there are pearls about its rim. Nine maidens guard it night and day. A liquid can be brewed in it. Whoever drinks of this becomes –

'Stop,' Morgant said quickly. 'That's enough now, Jamie. We haven't got all night.'

'I was interested.'

'Yes, well I can tell you about the Cauldron another time. That too is in Fintan's Tower, but it is not important.' He sighed. 'We must only think about the rescue; about Gweir.'

Jamie glanced at him curiously, at his small face, shadowy in the lamplight. It was that phrase in the Book. If the answer was lost in time, how long had this Gweir been in prison?

'Time,' Morgant said suddenly, as if guessing his thoughts, 'is a mystery. Each world has its own times and seasons.'

'Did you know Gweir?'

'Gweir is my brother.'

For a moment the room was cold. A draught moved the curtain and ruffled the pages of the Book, showing briefly that one of them was deep blue and covered with tiny, shining stars. Jamie held them still and turned back to look for it, but as he had guessed, it was gone.

'The Book gives nothing away,' Morgant remarked. 'Sit down, Gavan. Stop hanging over us like a cloud.'

The big man went round the table and flung himself on a chair. Jamie was glad. He quite liked Morgant but Gavan got on his nerves. Heavy and oppressive. A cloud was right; a storm cloud, full of threat.

'I still don't see what all this has to do with me,' he said aloud. 'Why is my name in here?'

'You were chosen; no one knows how. But it means, Jamie, that we need you to find Fintan's Tower.' Morgant made a small sweep with his hand. 'Will you come?'

'To the Harper's Beacon?'

'Apparently. And wherever the door leads.'

'To the "other worlds"?' Jamie shrugged. 'What does that mean?'

'There are dimensions within dimensions,' Morgant said dreamily. 'They lie behind each other like layers in mist; the world that is, the world that was, the world that might be. When the mist is around you, you can still see, although from a distance all is grey.'

Jamie was silent, thinking about it. Gavan gave him a leer. 'He's scared witless.'

'No,' Jamie said thoughtfully. 'I'm not. And I'm used to the hills. But won't it take much longer than a day?' He was wondering how the old man would manage on the steep wet slopes.

'Oh no. Maybe not so long. So that's agreed.' Morgant rubbed his hands together. 'Let us have something warming to celebrate.' He went to a small cupboard in the wall and brought back a tray with three glasses and a jug. The drink, when he poured it, was a ruby red.

'Something of my own. Not too strong.'

Jamie took a sip and coughed till the water came into his eyes. 'Very nice,' he managed.

The red-haired man downed his in one gulp and poured out more. Morgant tapped his hand. 'That's enough. We have work to do. Now, Jamie, listen to me. You must remember you are in great danger at every moment. This man Cai is out there, somewhere. He will not give up; you may not see him, but

24

he is both resourceful and cunning. Gavan will escort you home tonight.'

Jamie put the glass down again. 'I'd forgotten about him. Where does he come into it?'

'Obviously, he wants you to take him to the Tower, not us. He is a well-known thief,' Morgant said. 'I believe his aim is to steal the Cauldron of the King. It has certain . . . powers.'

Gavan snorted. 'Leave him to me.'

Morgant smiled. 'Now, on your way, Jamie.'

Halfway down the stairs Jamie paused. 'You haven't said when. And look, when we find your brother, well, he'll be guarded, won't he? They won't just hand him over.'

Morgant gave a quiet chuckle. 'The Book will advise us. As for when, the day after tomorrow, of course. Samain, when the doors of the Other world open. Allhallows Eve. We will meet at nine o'clock in the morning on Caston bridge, and be home before dark. We will see the sun's eye close and open.'

Then Jamie stepped out into the rain, and heard the bolts slam behind him.

Gavan hardly spoke all the way home. He walked huddled in his greatcoat and scarf, a huge shadow. Passers-by had to step off the pavement, as he wouldn't step aside. He didn't seem to care about cars either. Once, as he stepped into the road, a blue Volvo pulled up with a screech; the owner slammed his horn furiously but the big man just strode on, his eyes glittering in the lamplight. Warily Jamie kept an arm's length between them. Their footsteps rang loudly in the emptying streets. Sometimes he glanced behind, but the alleys and corners were dark and full of doorways. If anyone was there, he couldn't see them.

But half an hour later, when he was closing his bedroom curtains, he saw something that turned his skin damp. Opposite the house, in the doorway of the florist's, someone was standing. Who was it? He watched for a few minutes but the shadow did not move, and his feet were too cold to stay there. Puzzled, he let the curtain fall and climbed into bed.

Before he put the light out, he took the Book from under his pillow and opened it. 'Are you awake?'

Yes.

'The Tower. What is it, exactly?'

It is the Fortress of Frustration, the Fortress of Carousal. It is the Eerie Place.

'And this Cauldron, if you drink of it?'

If you drink from it you possess all knowledge.

'Worth stealing, then.'

Certainly.

And pondering that, he fell asleep.

5

In the Barn

'He's been there all morning.' Jamie's mother dropped the net curtain and went back to the stove. 'Just leaning against the wall.'

'Probably waiting for someone.' Mr Meyrick turned a page of the *Welsh Veterinary Bulletin* and wiped butter off it with his knife.

'For two hours? It's as if he's watching the house.' She broke an egg into the pan.

'Perhaps he's a policeman. Perhaps Jamie's robbed a bank.'

Jamie chewed his toast and kept his eyes on his book, but the words were a blur and his heart was beating so loudly he could hear it. 'What does he look like?' he asked quietly.

'Rather sinister.' Jennie had gone to see. 'Tall. Fair. Long black coat. A bit like a Russian spy, really.'

It was him. Once in the night Jamie had woken and lain awake, listening to soft footsteps under the window, up and down, in the silence of the street. But the Book's no good to him, he thought, panic rising inside. It's no good to him without me.

'What are you doing today?' his father asked, folding the paper and getting up. The stray puppy in his lap jumped down grumpily.

'Um . . . nothing much.'

'Good. I've got surgery all morning, so take a walk

out to the farm, will you? Your uncle's promised me a whole load of stuff – vegetables mostly – if we can collect it. Both of you could go.'

Jennie frowned. 'I'm supposed to be revising.'

'Ah, get on. You're daydreaming half the time.' Her father picked up his coat. 'Besides, the walk will do you good.'

Jamie bit his lip. He'd have to go – he didn't want to be left alone in the house – and the Book would have to come too. Leaving it would be too risky. But how could he get out, without Cai seeing, and following? He put down the astronomy book and went upstairs.

Gently, he moved a corner of curtain.

The stranger stood, leaning, arms folded, in the shadows of the alley opposite. He was looking up at the window, with a thin, sarcastic smile. Jamie jerked his hand back, then sat on the carpet and opened the Book. He was surprised at how cold he felt.

'Listen, how am I going to get out?'

The page was empty. No writing appeared.

'I'm asking!'

Use your initiative, the Book scrawled.

He closed it with a clap of disgust and went down to the kitchen.

His parents had gone. Jennie had her coat on, and was tucking the ends of her trousers into wellingtons.

'Those boots have got a hole in,' he told her absently.

'No, I had a go with the puncture kit. They'll be all right.' She took off her reading glasses and tugged the trimmed ends of hair off her face. 'Ready?'

'What about the washing-up?'

'Mam said she'd do it. She'll be back later.'

'Jen.' Jamie perched on the table. 'Let's go out the back way. Over the stream.'

'Why? We're going to the farm, idiot.'

'Yes I know, but . . .' Jamie pulled a face; would he really have to explain all this? 'It's that man out the front. He's . . . waiting for me, and I don't want him to see me. There was a scrap . . . a kid in school. That's his brother.'

Jennie took the clip out of her mouth and pushed it into her hair.

'You little thug. Have you told Dad?'

'No. And you mustn't either! Oh, come on, Jen, it won't take much longer.' He opened the back door. 'I just don't want all the fuss.'

'Coward. Infidel. Recreant knight.'

But she came with him, down the garden to the brook, which was flowing fast and cold this morning, after the rain, and littered with leaves. They splashed through and clambered up the opposite bank, through black brambles and bracken to the field at the top. There was a small gap in the hedge, made by pushing through it, year after year; beyond that was a ploughed field with a footpath along the edge. They followed the muddy track along the hedgerow, bright with haws, to the gate at the end; it wound along the bank of the stream to Caston Bridge, under a line of old willows with branches that stuck out like witches' hair. As they crossed the bridge Jamie looked down into the water rippling silently between the dark cutwaters. The field was an empty square of furrows. No one was following.

They threaded the alleys and lanes to the High Street, and waited impatiently to cross. Tourist coaches and lorries roared through the narrow street, whipping Jennie's hair into a whirlwind. She waved to a friend from school.

As they ran across, Jamie's eyes darted along the street. It was crammed with shoppers, but there was no sign of the tall, sinister figure. Surely he'd be easy to spot.

Colliding with a woman, he stammered an apology, almost dropped the Book, and was hauled by Jennie into Hanging Dog Lane. 'What did you do to that kid in school, anyway?' she asked, striding out in front. 'I wouldn't have thought you'd be much good in a fight. And can't you go anywhere without something to read!' He muttered something, uneasily. He had forgotten they would be coming this way.

Hanging Dog Lane was almost as dark as it had been the night before. Through the crack between the rooftops the sky was already grey with drizzle. They jumped down the steps and began to pass the small courtyards at each side. At the entrance to one Jamie stopped. 'Hang on a minute.'

He went down, over the cobbles. Maybe he should knock, and tell Morgant about the house being watched.

But the door was not there.

He stopped short, astonished, and glanced around. It was surely the same yard, with the rubbish bins and that poster flapping on the wall. But the doorway he had hidden in was gone; the dingy bricks were blank. He ran a hand over them, feeling their dampness. And the watchtower too! Above his head was just an ordinary roof, with two gulls screaming on a chimney.

'Come on, slug!' Jennie was watching him curiously. 'What's so special about that wall?'

'Nothing.' As he pushed past her he wondered what had happened to the world since the Book had come into it. Where had that room been, with its red and blue leaded windows? But after all, there was a maze of alleys in here; it may have been the wrong one. But he knew it wasn't.

The lane to the farm at Llanfihangell went slowly up a long steep hill; anyone following would have been easy to see on the black road. He and Jennie plodded on between the wet hedges, muffled up against the cold wind that blew in their faces; above them the sky was the colour of lead, stretching to the dark, huddled hills. Far up over the wood a buzzard swung on its wide, stiff wings.

Near the top of the hill a track branched off to the right, down through a plantation of fir trees to the farmhouse in its lonely hollow. Out of breath, Jamie paused and eased a corner of the Book that was digging into his ribs. Rain pattered loudly on his hood. He turned and glanced back, and saw, far behind, a small dark figure was striding up the lane.

Cold, Jamie clenched his fists. At this distance it could be anyone. He strained his eyes in the grey drizzle; there was something about that flapping coat and hurried step that terrified him. But how would he know? Jamie wondered. How could he? He turned and hurried after Jennie.

She was swishing the branches with a stick, and whistling. The track with its deep ruts wound its way down through the gloomy trees, and then with a twist that always surprised him, brought them out into the farmyard. The gates were shut, he noticed, and both the cars were gone.

'Hello! Anyone about?' Jennie poked her head into the outhouses and tried the back door. 'Bother. No one here, after all that trek. Shall we go in?'

Jamie was looking back up the track. 'Better. It's starting to rain.'

The key was in the soil under a stone under a flowerpot; trebly safe, Aunt Clare always said. They opened the door and found the kitchen dark and silent. Emperor, the big grey cat, was snoozing on a sofa by the sinking fire. The table was a clutter of bills and papers and on the mantelpiece was a note written in blue eyebrow pencil:

Jennie. Your mother phoned to say you were coming. Fruit and veg. in kitchen. Potatoes in the barn. Lock up after you.

'She's gone to Abergavenny,' Jenny realized. 'To the market.' She went into the kitchen and began opening cupboards.

Jamie put some logs on the fire and sat down; the cat climbed thoughtfully on to his lap. He turned over the newspaper on the table – there was a paragraph headed ECLIPSE. He read it carefully.

. . . As readers of our regular Astronomy column will know, there will be a total eclipse of the sun on Saturday afternoon, 31 October, beginning at approximately 12.30 p.m. and lasting until within minutes of sunset, although the actual time of totality will be only two minutes. The eclipse will be visible from the whole of Wales and is already attracting interest from occult groups as well as astronomers, because it takes place on Hallowe'en, the ancient magical night of Samain. According to local white witch Ceridwen Hughes, this is the night when the barriers between the natural and the supernatural worlds grow thin, and ghosts, demons and faeries walk our roads and woods . . .

'Potatoes!' Jennie shouted from the kitchen. 'Get them, will you?'

> . . . and, she says, it is a time of great danger and peril to anyone out after dark. So all you astronomers beware!

'Jamie! Come on!'

He dropped the paper with a sigh, and heaved the cat aside. So that was what the Book meant by the sun's eye closing. He might have guessed it was something like that. And 'white witch Ceridwen Hughes' certainly cheered you up.

A gust of wind snatched the door from his hand and flung rain in his face; he ran, coat huddled on, over the slippery cobbles of the yard, through the stable and the downpour from its corrugated roof, into the barn. The door swung behind him.

The barn was dim, and quiet. Water dripped here and there from the roof; it smelt of straw, and tar, and the autumnal earth.

The potatoes were at one side, stacked in sacks; he waded through the straw towards them. The sound of the rain was hushed; he could hear the pigeons shuffling outside, and the faint squeak of a mouse in the stacked bales. As he hauled out a sack, there was a rustle in the dimness at the far end of the loft. He stopped, the hairs on the backs of his hands prickling with sudden alarm.

'Who's there?' he said quietly. The rafters creaked. The echoes of his question hung in the air like dust. For a long moment he waited, listening intently to every tiny sound. Rain spattered under the door; a tin can rattled over the cobbles outside. In the barn, nothing moved. But suddenly Jamie could see him.

It wasn't much, just a shadow in the dimness, quite still, but it was a man's shoulder and arm, black in the blackness. He kept his eyes on it, backing away noiselessly, feeling his scalp prickle and grow hot with each step. Straw rustled as his feet passed through it. Then the shadow moved. 'Jamie,' it said.

Jamie turned, slammed through the door, hurtled across the wet yard and burst into the kitchen. 'Jennie!' he yelled breathlessly, pulling the bolts across. 'He's there! He's in the barn!'

He whirled around and the words died in his mouth. Jennie was sitting in the armchair by the fire. Leaning against the table, with his arms folded and his mocking dark eyes turned to look at him, was the the third man from the library.

6

Cai

For a moment there was silence. Then the man said, 'Don't make a fuss. Come in and sit down.'

His voice was quiet, with a soft, old-fashioned accent. Moving to the nearest chair, Jamie glanced at Jennie. He was relieved to see her glaring back at him. 'Fight! There's a lot more to this than a fight,' she muttered. 'Will someone tell me what's going on?'

The stranger ignored her. 'You're a difficult person to get to talk to, Jamie,' he said. 'Put the Book on the table.'

Jamie hesitated. The man was leaning casually against the table, hands deep in the pockets of his dark coat. He seemed to have no weapons. If I ran, Jamie thought . . .

'Don't be stupid. You wouldn't even get to the door.'

Cai straightened; Jamie was shocked at how tall he seemed. His eyes were cold and amused. 'Put the Book down,' he snapped, 'or I'll take it myself.'

It seemed to have gone very dark in the room. The fire crackled over the new logs, and the cat licked itself contentedly. Jamie pulled the Book from his inside pocket and laid it, carefully, on Aunt Clare's check tablecloth. It was in a bag because of the rain; drops of moisture slid down one corner and soaked into the material.

The tall man smiled, bleakly. 'Well, that's a start.'

'It's no good to you without me.'

'So you know that much.'

'Yes.' Jamie rolled up his fists. 'And I'm not asking it anything for you.'

Cai shrugged; his eyes narrowed. 'I can see they've told you all about me. I might have known.'

With a sudden snatch like a striking snake, he had hold of Jamie's arm. 'But then I need to know where Fintan's Tower is.' He tugged the Book from its cover and flicked it open. 'Ask it! Or have they done that already?' He grinned at Jamie's scared look. 'Yes, of course they have. Morgant never did waste any time.'

Jamie glanced at Jennie. Her face was white and bewildered, but her hands were moving under the table. Slowly, inch by inch, she was opening the drawer where the knives and forks were kept. He squirmed in the man's grip. 'Let me go! You can't make me tell you anything!'

'Oh no?' Cai dropped his arm and stood back.

Jamie rubbed his aching wrist angrily. 'You're a thief!'

A spark of surprise and fury kindled in the man's face. He glanced at Jennie, who froze, and then back to Jamie. 'I didn't want this. But if you're going to be that stubborn . . .'

Suddenly, he raised his hands. The air crackled, grew hot, and Jennie gasped. Between his narrow fingers a ring of light hung in the air, and as his hands moved slowly apart the ring widened; became a clear, spinning circle of white fire blazing in the centre of the room. Jamie stared at it, fascinated by the pure emptiness; it was as if a circle had been cut out of the air, and he could see through.

At first the whiteness was unbroken – then, all at once, something was in there. It was a landscape of fields and trees, not a still picture but a real place, as if he was looking at it through a peephole, or a circular window. It was raining there too; the sky was steel-grey and he could see storm clouds piling up over the hills. In the foreground was a lake, its cold ripples lapping the shingle; and out on the mist, as if it rose out of the water, he could see a great fortress glimmering in the dull light. Flickers of lightning played silently over the waves. He had seen it before; it had been tiny then, in bright enamels on the Book's cover, but here it was huge, rain-lashed, gleaming wet, with one lighted window high up near the battlements. This was Fintan's Tower, and the way to it lay through the door on the Harper's Beacon, when the sun's eye was closed.

He did not hear himself say the words. When he could hear at all it was only somebody laughing, and a voice shouting, 'Jamie! Jamie!' over and over. His sight cleared; Jennie was shaking his shoulders. He was cold and rigid and stiff; the white ring was gone and it was Cai who was smiling, his strange shining hair falling over his eyes.

'You told him!' Jennie said. 'Whatever he wanted, you told him. Are you all right?' She gripped his arm again and shook it; he saw the handle of the knife in her sleeve.

'Yes . . . yes. I'm OK.' He fought the strange confusion away and glared at the man over her shoulder. 'All right! So now you know. Now clear out and leave us alone!'

The man shook his head, still grinning. 'It's not that easy. I'm taking this with me.' He picked up the Book and closed it carefully. 'And as you were bright enough to point out, it's useless without you. So you'll have to come as well.'

Jennie stiffened. From the corner of his eye Jamie saw the handle of the knife slide down into her palm.

Cai lounged against the table. 'She can stay here. Come on, Jamie, don't make it too much work for me. You've seen what I can do.' But he stopped as Jennie turned round. She held the knife out firmly; the sharp edge of it glittered in the firelight.

'Listen,' she said, in a cold harsh voice that Jamie barely recognized, 'I don't know who you are, and I don't know what that Book thing is all about. But my brother and I are going home. Now. So please get out of my way.'

The stranger's face flushed with rage; for a moment he looked so angry that he couldn't speak. Jennie grabbed her brother's arm.

'Come on.'

'Wait!' Cai jerked forward. He seemed to be forcing himself to keep his temper. 'Wait. Listen to me. Have they told you what is in the tower?'

'You mean the Cauldron?'

His eyes narrowed. 'You know about that!'

'All about it.'

Jennie tugged him towards the door, but Cai leapt after them.

'Put that stupid thing down!' he stormed. 'You're not going to use it.'

'I will!'

Furiously the man lashed a chair out of his way. 'Will you let me explain!'

'You don't need to, I know all about it!' Jamie yelled. 'I know about the Prisoner and the Cauldron and all about you!' And he tugged the last stiff bolt back from the door.

'No! Come here!' The man flung himself forward and grabbed Jamie's arm. 'Listen . . .' Suddenly he

38

swore and stumbled back, clutching his hand. Blood welled from a deep cut across his knuckles. 'You little vixen!'

'I'm sorry, really I am.' Jennie was white and shaky; Jamie could feel her trembling. 'But you should have left us alone!' She slid the knife on to the table and then picked it up again.

The man gave her a shrewd look; his temper had vanished. Quickly he snatched a white handkerchief from a pile of Aunt Clare's ironing and tied it round his hand; a crimson stain flushed slowly through the fabric. Then he glanced at them and said quietly, 'Did you never think it might all be lies, Jamie, all those things they told you?'

His hand on the latch, Jamie paused.

'They told you they want to rescue Gweir, didn't they? Well, it's a lie.'

'Open the door, Jamie,' Jennie said quickly.

'Listen to me, Jamie! They want the Cauldron for themselves. That's all. They don't care about the Prisoner, they'd leave him there to rot! They're using you to get what they want!'

Slowly, Jamie let the door swing open. A gust of wind swept in and crackled the flames in the hearth. Then he turned around and faced Cai. 'But *you* want the Cauldron.'

'No! At least . . .' A flicker of something passed over the man's face. 'No. I don't.'

Jamie shook his head. 'I don't believe you,' he said. 'After all, you would say that.'

'Of course he would!' Gavan blocked the doorway, his head brushing the lintel, his great coat flapping like a cloak. He brought a huge heavy hand down on Jamie's shoulder. 'Out! Go home. I'll take care of this.' Roughly, he bundled them both out of the door.

'So Morgant's sent his little lapdog, has he?' Cai smiled in cold fury. 'How pleasant! How enchanting!'

Ignoring him, Gavan glared down at Jamie. 'Clear out,' he growled, jerking his head towards the lane.

But even with Jennie tugging him, Jamie held back. 'I can't. He's got the Book.'

Like a bear, Gavan swung back, his arms hanging loosely at his sides. Cai lounged against the table. 'Oh dear, now you've confused him. That's a lot for him to take in. Is this your idea of a generous rescuer, Jamie?'

'Let's have it,' Gavan growled.

He lurched forward.

'Careful.' Cai's voice was soft and lazy. 'Remember what happened to Palug's Cat.'

The Book lay between them on the table. Suddenly, before anyone could move, Jamie darted under Gavan's arm, ran across the kitchen and snatched it up. The room exploded into sparks of white flame; the shape in his hands writhed and buckled and burnt him. Then he staggered back, dazzled.

Cai was gone. The room was empty but for a faint, fragrant smoke and the Book, hot and smoking in his hands.

'Stupid thing to do!' Gavan muttered, pushing past him to look around. 'He could have killed you. I would have got the Book, without that.'

'Yes, but where did he *go*?' Jennie came in and stared at the table.

'Oh, he's up to all sorts of tricks.' Gavan shrugged 'Notorious for it. Cunning as a snake. I suppose you didn't tell him anything?'

His small red eyes fixed suddenly on Jamie.

'Well . . . he knows where Fintan's Tower is – at

least, what the Book said.' Alarmed at the man's face, he added, 'Well, he *made* me tell him!'

The big man stormed over and kicked the door open furiously. 'Made you! You've got legs, haven't you! You could run!'

'Yes, but . . .'

'Oh, save it.' Gavan threw an evil look over his shoulder. 'Save it for the old man. And he won't like it either. Not one bit.'

7
Eclipse

Jennie sat back against the tree and gazed at the brook flowing past her feet. A shaft of late sunlight slanted through the leaves on to the water, lighting up the tiny stones and gravel, and the flash of a fin. Leaves swept by on the current like small leathery coracles.

'You had a lot of nerve,' Jamie said, 'with that knife.'

'Mmm.' She threw a stone in, thoughtfully. 'So that's it. It's all a very odd story. And you say this Book actually tells you things? That's impossible. It's some kind of trick.'

'I thought so at first, but it's not. I'll show you.' Jamie opened the Book at random on his knees and asked it the first question that came into his head. 'Who is this man Cai, anyway?'

The Emperor's foster brother, the Book wrote.

'Wow.' Jennie touched the page with her finger. 'Impressive. What Emperor?'

'Tell her,' Jamie said.

Arthur, of course. Cai is a Master of Fire and Water. He can last nine nights without sleep. A wound from his sword no one can heal. He fought nine witches: they say he laughed as he slew them. He is a Harper, a Smith, an Enchanter. He killed Palug's Cat.

'Palug's Cat?'

Yes. Nine score warriors would fall as her food.

Jennie giggled. 'It talks in riddles!'

'Oh, you get used to that.' He read the page again. 'I don't like the sound of this. He scares me.'

'Well, if he killed some kind of leopard that tucked into, um, 180 people as a light lunch, then he's no joke. As we know. Look, Jamie, seriously, I'm coming on this jaunt. If Fintan's Tower is real, I want to see it. You'll need help. And,' she muttered quietly, 'I know he's on your side, but I don't like that thug Gavan, either.'

Jamie watched the kitten dipping its paw into the stream. He'd known she would say that. And in a way he was glad, because he didn't like Gavan either. It made you think . . .

'You know, back there, at the farm,' he said, 'if Gavan hadn't have come in . . .'

'What?'

'Well, I almost – for a moment – believed him. Cai, I mean. What if Morgant is stringing us along?'

Jennie shrugged. 'One of them must be lying.'

'Mmm.' After a moment he turned to a clean page and said, 'Listen, what does Morgant really want? Does he want to rescue Gweir?'

The Book drew a complicated scroll. Then, inside, it wrote:

Who knows the secrets of men's hearts?

The next morning they were ten minutes early at Caston Bridge. The street outside the house had been empty, but then Cai already knew where they were going. The wind had been rising all night, and they had dressed warmly in pullovers and waterproofs. Jennie had brought some sandwiches and a flask of hot tea; these were in a small rucksack with the Book. 'We take turns to carry this, mind,' she had said, loosening the strap against her shoulder.

Now, she kicked her boot impatiently against the stones of the bridge. 'I'm freezing! Where are they?'

'Here.' Jamie saw them turn the corner, the small old man with his hands in his pockets; Gavan with the canvas bag under his arm. They were talking, Gavan's head bent down to listen. Then they laughed.

'Is that him?' Jennie said in a low voice.

'Yes.' Jamie frowned. 'Keep alert, Jen. I want to know what's really going on.'

As he came up, Morgant stopped in mock surprise. 'What's this? Two of you?'

'If she can't come, I won't either,' said Jamie, firmly.

'Tut, nonsense.' Morgant smiled. 'Just my little joke. I wouldn't dream of sending you back, my dear; Gavan told me about your adventure yesterday. It was a very brave thing to do, if you don't mind me saying so.'

'I don't know,' Jennie said. 'I was just scared.'

Morgant nodded. 'He is a dangerous man. He will be angry now, and we will have to be even more careful. It's a great pity he managed to find out so much.' He smiled then, and his small black eyes gleamed at them. 'Now then. We have to be at Harper's Beacon by noon. Shall we go?'

They crossed the bridge and followed the road out of town, turning off into a muddy lane that would take them up into the hills. At the turning Jamie couldn't help looking back, but the bridge was empty, and the street deserted.

It was a long walk, through the rustling end-of-autumn countryside and the mild, damp air. They travelled mostly along footpaths and wet, rutted tracks that climbed slowly towards the grey bulk of the hills; the Mynydd Maen they were called. Harper's Beacon was a great mound on the end of the range, made no one knew when; an old barrow, some said, or a motte with deep ditches. A circle of standing stones crowned it, grey and leaning in the wind. Once, resting against a tree for breath and glancing up there, Jamie was sure he could make out tiny figures moving around among the stones. He shouted to Morgant, who came hurrying back.

'Ah yes.' Morgant took a telescope from his bag and focused it carefully on the hill top. 'Yes, well, I expected this, of course. The path of the total eclipse is not that broad, you see. Every hill on it will have observers – people watching, you know. Astronomers. The higher up, the better for them – clear air, and so on. They won't make any difference to us. They won't see what we're looking for.'

'The Fortress of Frustration?'

Morgant threw him a quick glance. 'I see you've been making enquiries of your own.'

'A few. It doesn't explain much, though.'

Morgant smiled. 'Only if you know what to ask. But we won't find the Fortress up there, remember. Just the door.'

Puzzled, Jamie watched him walk on towards Gavan, who was idling impatiently along the lane. Jennie nudged his back. 'Carry this for a bit. It's your turn.'

It was harder to walk with the rucksack on. After a

45

few more miles he was plodding and daydreaming, head down. They were climbing steadily now, up the lower slopes of the hills, stopping every now and then to catch their breath. Below them the countryside spread itself, golds, russets and greens. They could see great woods, dappled brown and red as the few leaves left on the trees crinkled and decayed. The hedgerows were speckled with berries, and on a ploughed field in the valley a crowd of lapwings and gulls followed a single yellow tractor.

Gavan, at a signal from Morgant, began to keep dawdling behind, peering into bushes and copses at the side of the lanes. Once Morgant looked back and Jamie saw Gavan slightly shake his head. Jennie had noticed too. 'They're looking for him,' she whispered.

Jamie nodded. 'I know. And what's the use? He could be up there watching us come.'

The last part of the climb went up a steep, stony track between hedges of blackthorn and stunted oak, all bending one way in the bitter wind. The track was full of puddles. Jamie splashed through them, his chest aching for breath, the wind in his face becoming colder. Then they climbed a stile, and stood on the springy turf of the open hill. Above them, bare rock jutted out, and they clambered up over it, down into ditches scraped red by rabbits, through the snagging, coconut-smelling bushes of yellow gorse, until they stood up breathless on the bare, eroded mound of the Harper's Beacon.

The wind struck them like a roaring wave. Coat flapping, Jamie stared out at the hills, miles of them, briefly stroked with light as the sun broke through the fine cloud. Ebbw forest, all moving shadow, and beyond that the mountains of Powys and Hereford-shire, in the dim blueness of the horizon.

'Look at that!' Jennie shouted. Her hair streamed out behind her, whipping itself into fantastic shapes.

Jamie nodded, and turned.

Behind him the stones of the prehistoric circle rose like a crown on the hill top, gaunt and ominous.

They took shelter from the wind in the ditch; there were about a dozen people there already, setting up telescopes and expensive-looking cameras. Around the stones some hippies squatted, colourfully dressed; one girl was singing to the sound of a flute. Jamie couldn't help wondering if she was white witch Ceridwen Hughes.

'Quite a crowd,' Morgant observed. He drew them away to the seclusion of some large rocks, and sat down.

Gavan took a flask from his pocket, unscrewed it, and took a long, noisy drink.

'Now,' said the old man, straightening his legs with a sigh, 'the Book, Jamie. I think I know what will happen, but we must be sure.'

Swallowing a mouthful of cheese sandwich, Jamie pulled the Book out and opened it. He stared with surprise. The page was covered with a picture of a wolf, its snarling head turned to him, yellow eyes glaring fiercely. For a second he was sure he caught his own reflection in those eyes; then the wind ruffled the paper.

'Turn back!' Jennie gasped, and he did, but there was no sign of the picture.

'What was it?'

'Hmm.' Morgant put the tips of his fingers together. 'Interesting. I'm not sure. But ask it about the Tower, Jamie.'

Jamie crouched out of the wind. 'We're on the Harper's Beacon,' he said, feeling like someone on the radio. 'What now?'

> *Wait*, the Book wrote. *Wait until the sun's eye is fully closed. You will see between two stones the door into the Summer Country. Pass through it and come back before the sun's eye opens even a little. You have only the twinkling of an eye.*

'You mean while the total eclipse is happening?' Jamie shook his head. 'That's impossible. The sun is only blotted out fully for two minutes. How can we go in, find the Tower, rescue the Prisoner and get back in two minutes!'

The Book did not answer.

'Time,' said Morgant, 'moves differently. I warned you. Once in the Summer Country we might have days, or even weeks, while here it is just the twinkling of an eye.'

They were silent a moment. Then Jennie said, 'Well, if I'd known, I'd have brought a change of socks.'

The eclipse began on time; the cloud had been hazy but began to clear to the west. It was too dangerous to look directly at the sun, but one of the men nearby let Jamie look through his telescope, which had a coloured filter on. 'You need that,' the man told him. 'Look at it without that and it could blind you.'

It was a peculiar sight. The sun was a pale globe, a lemon balloon with dirty spots on it, and something had already begun to take a bite out of one side. Infinitely slowly, the black disc of the moon was creeping across. It took over an hour; he and Jennie took it in turns to watch, fascinated by that rolling blackness.

48

Morgant observed carefully, taking notes in his spidery handwriting; Gavan sat huddled in his greatcoat, slumped out of the wind, drinking and dozing. Once or twice he got up and stamped about, to the annoyance of the astronomers.

Soon, even without the telescope, they could see it was getting darker. The sky slowly became deep blue and dusky, and a chill breeze sprang up round the rocks, flapping papers and clothes. The hippies formed a ring and began to circle, hand in hand among the stones. Carefully, Jamie packed the Book away. The sun was a pale crescent now, dwindling quickly. Around him cameras were clicking, and people were murmuring in excitement.

'All my life,' muttered the man with the telescope to his neighbour, 'all my life I've been waiting for this.'

Second by second, the sun's eye was closing. Light narrowed to a sliver; shadows stood out sharply on the ground, so that each blade of grass had its own, and those of the standing stones were black. Birdsong stopped, as if the birds thought night had come, and the lights in the houses down the valley began to flicker on.

And then, from the east, Jamie saw it coming, the black shadow of the moon racing towards him over the countryside, hurtling over the woods and villages and up the slope of the hills until it swept over his face in perfect silence, and the sun went out.

In the stillness, they stared upwards. The sky was full of stars. The sun was black, and around it great tongues of fire flickered, an eerie glow flaring out like the petals of a ghostly flower. Cameras whirred and clicked. Someone chuckled in the silence.

Jamie felt a tap on his shoulder and turned,

impatiently, from the awe of the sky. Morgant pushed him towards the mound. 'Look.'

In the strange, purple dimness the two nearest stones were black, and between them in the air something shimmered and twisted, hardly seen. Through it there was a deeper darkness. Without a word he scrambled up beside Morgant and watched as Gavan stretched his arm out into the shimmer, and saw how it dissolved and disappeared. Gavan slid into the emptiness. One by one, silent as shadows, they followed him, slipping between the stones and vanishing into darkness. Jamie was last. He took one last look at the black sun, and stepped through.

'Here, son, take a look.' The man with the telescope tore his eyes from the sun and glanced around. 'Where did they go?' he asked his neighbour. The neighbour shrugged, showing a glint of bright hair under his dark hood. 'Who knows?'

But in half a second he had gone too.

There

Tri lloneit prytwen yd aetham ni idi
Nam seith ny dyrreith o gaer sidi . . .

Three shiploads of Prydwen we went into it;
Save seven none returned from the Faery
Fortress . . .

The Spoils of Annwn

8

The Black Wood

Jamie stepped between the two stones and almost fell into someone's waiting hands.

'Keep still!' Gavan muttered in his ear. 'It's dark here.'

It certainly was. Even the wan eclipse light was gone; in this place it was cold, and black, utterly black. He felt Jennie shiver next to him. 'Where are we?' she asked.

There was a crisp splutter and a blue flare came out of the darkness, lighting Morgant's small face and beard. He bent and lit a lantern from his pack and waited till the light turned yellow and steadied. An oily smell came through the darkness, and mixed with it the sharp scent of pine needles and wet bark.

'We're in a wood,' Morgant said after a moment. He moved the lamp about carefully, and they glimpsed black branches silhouetted against his face. 'Yes. The trees are thickly crowded.'

Jamie looked up. A black interlace of twigs webbed across the sky; he could hear the thick canopy rustling softly, and through it caught the gleam of starlight. Wherever they were, it was deep midnight.

From their left came a great crashing and crackling; something seemed to be forcing its way through the undergrowth. Then Gavan's voice came from a distance: 'Over here. It's clearer this way.'

They followed, stumbling blindly over logs and

brambles. Jamie was last; as he moved he caught a whisper of sound behind him and whipped round. His yell of fright brought Jennie and Morgant scrambling back.

'He was there!'

'Are you sure?'

'It must have been him. Just a shadow, reaching out . . .'

'All right,' Morgant said quietly. He raised his voice; it came out of the dark and echoed strangely among the invisible, crowding trees. 'Can you hear me, Cai Wyn?'

The wood rustled, but there was no answer.

'All this patience will do you no good,' Morgant went on calmly. 'If you come too close, no one will reach Fintan's Tower. I'm sure you know what I mean by that.'

The forest was silent. Then, not far off, someone laughed.

'Look out, Jamie.' Cai's voice came softly out of the darkness. 'Remember what I said.'

Morgant jerked them away. 'Come on. He's too close.'

It took them about ten minutes to struggle to a clearer part of the wood, and with the noise they made, Jamie thought, anyone could have followed them. His eyes began to get used to the darkness; once in the clearing, he could make out the tall tree-shapes crowding round, and the wet grass glittering in the starlight. It was the stars that astonished him most. 'They're all wrong,' he muttered to Jennie. They were bright, and scattered like glittering dust in peculiar patterns.

'Look at your watch, Jamie.' Morgant was beside him; as they walked he tugged up his sleeve.

'But that was the time the eclipse started! It's stopped.' The faintly green hands stood still at two minutes to three.

Morgant chuckled. 'It hasn't stopped – not quite. If you watched it for a few hours you might see it move a second. But each one is long, very long.'

'So we have the two minutes of the eclipse – until my watch shows three o'clock?'

'Exactly.'

'And that might be days?'

'Who knows?'

'And what happens if we don't get back in time? ' Jennie asked quickly.

'Well, that would be very unfortunate. Who knows when the door would be open again, mm?' In the dimness behind the lantern Gavan chortled. Morgant ignored him. 'But it won't happen. We have plenty of time. Now, this seems to be a path of sorts. Perhaps we should enquire of the Book?'

But the Book just wrote *Get out of the wood* in a laconic scrawl across the page, yellow in the lamplight.

'I think we woke it up,' Jennie giggled.

Following the path in the darkness was not easy. Morgant went first with the dull star of the lantern in his hand, lighting the undergrowth and throwing black, leaping shadows against the boles of trees. Jennie walked behind him, then Jamie, his thumbs under the chafing straps of the rucksack. Gavan came last, noisily, the canvas bag tucked effortlessly under one arm. Behind him, the wood was silent.

The path began to slope steeply down, winding between the damp tree trunks. They slithered and clattered over slippery stones as they walked, and sometimes had to use their hands to scramble over rocks, or had to squelch through sudden patches of deep mud. Gavan stumbled along clumsily, often treading on Jamie's heels, sometimes stopping and staring back. But the path remained a dark notch between the trees. Wherever he is, Jamie thought, with a delight that surprised himself, wherever he is, *you* won't see him.

Gradually, the sky grew lighter, and the stars faded. But the wood stayed silent; there was no birdsong, or rustle of small animals. It puzzled Jamie when he noticed it. And in the growing light he could see the trees along the path were beeches, but their trunks and bare branches were black, as if a great fire had swept through the wood and charred it. It was a desolation; no leaves, no buds. A wood of black, twisted shapes.

There was no sunrise. The dull light grew around them, revealing a grey sky faintly tinged with copper. When it was quite light Jamie glanced back up the rocky path behind him and found it empty. Alarmed, he called the others, and they waited for Gavan to catch up. When he came he was smirking.

Morgant glared at him. 'Where have you been? We should keep together.'

The big man grinned. 'Just been making a few arrangements. For our sarcastic friend.' He pulled a coil of rope out of the bag and showed it to them. 'A few little accidents to slow him down.'

Morgant smiled; Jamie looked at Jennie. He felt uneasy,and the feeling was growing the further they went.

As she turned, Jennie pointed down the track. 'Look. The light is different.'

They walked on and found that the wood ended suddenly, and before them lay an immense grassy plain, rising, it seemed, to a distant horizon. Nothing moved except the grass, bending and whispering in the breeze. There were no birds. The coppery sky was still and ominous.

'I suppose we have to cross this?'

'I fear so,' Morgant said thoughtfully. 'There's no telling how far the Tower may be. Perhaps just over this plain. But let's sit for a while and eat, shall we, here at the edge of the trees. It seems we have a long walk ahead.'

He nodded curtly to Gavan, who tossed their bag down and flung himself beside it. Jennie sat down next to Jamie. 'How's the time?'

'Oh, fine. Took us three seconds to get this far.'

'In that case,' Morgant mused, 'we may only have two or three days. It's less than I had hoped.'

Jennie shook her head. 'It's weird. Look at this place. No birds. No sounds. Not even any sun. Just grass.'

The loneliness of the scene rolled over them as they ate; the grasses swished themselves in the slight breeze. Jennie finished the last sandwich, then poured out the dregs of the tea, screwed up the flask and put it back in the rucksack. Never mind socks, Jamie thought, they should have brought much more food.

Suddenly Morgant said, 'Jamie, I have an idea. It would be safer, you know, if you gave the Book to somebody else to carry. At the moment, if our enemy should make some attempt to abduct you – and he well might – he'd get both you and the Book. I think we should split you up.'

The idea chilled Jamie. He knew it made sense, but it increased his uneasiness.

'Jennie can carry it then,' he said, after a moment.

'No,' Morgant said quietly. 'No. I think I should. That would be best.'

In the silence the grasses swished. Jamie laughed, awkwardly. 'Yes, but I'm the one whose name is in it. Doesn't that mean – '

'Come on!' Gavan growled. 'Do as he says!'

'It's only common sense,' Morgant added. 'I'm sure you think so, Jennie?'

'I don't know.' She fiddled with her shoelaces and threw a frown at Jamie. He could tell she didn't like this. 'No . . . I don't want to.'

Morgant made a swift sign; at once Gavan grabbed the rucksack and pulled the Book out.

'Hey!' Jamie jumped up, but the big man shoved him back and tossed the Book to Morgant.

'Thank you. Now it's really for the best, Jamie. We can't lose both you and it.'

Furious, Jamie watched the Book vanish into the bag. Morgant did the straps up tidily and then stood up. 'And now for another brisk walk. Follow me.'

And he strode off through the grass.

At first Jamie lagged behind, trying to get a quiet word with Jennie, but Gavan kept too close. Jamie was furious with himself, and very worried. Up until now he hadn't realized how reassuring the Book had been; without it he felt strangely alone, and rather helpless. Distrust nagged at him. Did Morgant want it just to keep it safe? Or to keep him? He began to wonder about them. Where had they come from, after all? What did he really know? Everything they had told him could be a lie.

Brooding, he thrashed through the grass. It seemed to go on for ever; a sea of soft swishing around their waists. When he looked back, the wood was already a low black huddle on the horizon; on either side as far as he could see, the flat grasslands filled the world. How could Cai follow them over this? He'd be seen, surely – or was he subtle enough to crouch and run and merge with the ripples of colour and shadow? Or perhaps Gavan's trap had stopped him. Jamie remembered the farm, the man's cut hand, his anger. If he was badly hurt he might be more dangerous, ready to leap up from the grass any minute. But somehow, Jamie had begun to suspect that would not happen.

On and on the grasses waved around them. They plodded silently through the long hours of the morning. When the voice came, it seemed to wake them from sleep.

'Travelling far, strangers?'

Jamie's head jerked up; Gavan swore and spun round.

A man sat in the grass, half-hidden. He had a brown, dirty, pleasant face and straggly hair; his clothes were a patchwork of browns and greens. Behind him a small grey donkey grazed.

'Where did you spring from?' roared Gavan. Jamie knew that if the man had not spoken, they would not even have noticed him.

The brown man laughed. 'I asked first,' he said.

'We seek Fintan's Tower.' Morgant came back and looked at him with interest.

'Indeed? Well, just keep walking, friend. Fintan's Tower stands before you.'

The way he said it made Jamie feel it was right there, but when he turned his head there was only empty grass to the horizon.

The man smiled; it seemed to annoy Morgant. 'Thank you,' he said abruptly, and turned and walked on.

The stranger eyed Jamie and Jennie. 'I think I know you,' he said. 'Jamie.'

Astonished, Jamie stared. 'How did you know my name?'

The man winked. 'Ah. And what's your business at the Fortress? Are you in any need?'

'Well . . .' Jamie looked round furtively, 'I think we might be – '

'That's enough! Our business is our business.' Gavan pushed them both in front of him hurriedly.

'Hey!' Jennie said angrily. 'Don't shove!'

But catching their arms with a grip like a vice, he pulled them away.

Looking back, Jamie saw the man still sitting there, watching, and chewing a blade of grass. He raised a hand, with a mocking sort of smile. Soon the grass hid him from sight.

That afternoon the weather worsened. Low dark clouds rolled over; it began to drizzle, and then to rain heavily. Soaked through and hungry they stumbled on, into the coppery dimness that was closing round. Lightning flickered once or twice, and thunder rumbled far off in the west, the echoes rolling for miles over the endless tundra.

They became shadows to each other: dark shapes in the falling rain. It was only after one blue crash of lightning that the shadow that was Morgant stopped suddenly, arms wide to keep them back. They clustered around him, and saw that at his feet the plain ended, and a cliff, seamed with ravines and shattered rock, plummeted into darkness. And there, far out in the invisible country beyond, one tiny light flickered and shone in the rain, a white, pure spark like a star, and it might have been nearby, or miles away . . . they couldn't tell.

'Look,' said Morgant. 'That light is on Fintan's Tower.'

9

Down the Cliff

'It's for your own good,' Morgant said again.

Jennie fingered the end of the rope. 'I don't want to. Why should we be tied in pairs? If one falls he'll pull the other down. It's a crazy idea.'

'Stop whining and tie it on!' In the rain Gavan's temper had worsened. 'Why did we bring her?' he yelled at Morgant. 'We don't need her!' His small eyes bulged; rain plastered his hair to his face.

'Shut up,' Morgant barked. 'Tie it on, girl, and hurry. The rocks are slippery now, and this rain will make it worse. You will be with me and your brother with Gavan. We need to keep together.'

White-faced, Jennie tied on the rope. She flung a look at Jamie and hissed, 'I *hate* them!'

He bit his lip. She was right; they should never have come. Morgant knew. He knew they suspected him; knew as well as they did that the ropes weren't for safety, but to keep them prisoner. For all his sticky politeness, all Morgant wanted was for them to get him to the Tower. And it was too late to break free.

Gavan swung himself over the cliff edge; they heard him scrabble about on the wet rocks. 'All right,' he yelled, his head suddenly reappearing. 'It's not bad. Rocky ledges and a narrow path.'

He vanished again. Jamie climbed down carefully, and Jennie followed. Morgant was last. The wind flung rain at them, their numb fingers slipped on the stones. In the growing darkness each step was a danger; scree slithered about under their feet, and small showers of stones trickled and clattered down on to rocks far below. How high the cliff was it was impossible to tell, but it seemed very high to Jamie. Behind him, he heard Morgant slip and cling and curse.

There was a path of sorts, but it was broken and disused. Often it vanished altogether, and they clung to narrow toeholds and knobs and corners of rock. The rain swept across the miles of dark land below and slapped them against the cliff; water ran from above in trickles and torrents down their sleeves and into their hair, soaking them to the skin. Twice they had to leap dark empty clefts in the rock, toes stretching out over nothing, only half-seeing the other side.

But it was on an easy stretch of the path that Jamie heard Jennie shriek behind him; he turned to run, but the rope held him tight. 'Gavan!' he screamed. 'Wait!'

The big man wiped rain out of his eyes, but instead of turning back he leaned against a rock, grinning. Quite suddenly Jamie was afraid. The rope was looped around his waist; he tore it over his head and turned. Far up the slope Jennie was shouting – but before he had gone two steps, Gavan was on him.

Jamie bit and struggled but, laughing, Gavan held him, huge arms like a bear's tight around his chest, till, savage with fury, Jamie brought his heel down and stamped, hard, on the man's foot. Gavan roared, and staggered back, lost balance; and with a shove Jamie was free, and racing up the steep track. He hurtled round a rock and flung himself flat on the stones, grabbing at the rope that was slithering over the edge. In a flicker of lightning he saw Jennie's hands, and then her face, white in the blackness as she hung on to the loosening branches, hauling herself up. She screamed and slipped, but before the rumble of the thunder came he had grabbed her arm and was pulling, heaving her weight towards him. Rain beat in his face and blinded him. Then she was kneeling next to him, breathless, on the narrow, streaming path, staring at Morgant, who had watched it all and had not moved an inch.

'You just stood there!' she yelled, as soon as she could speak. 'I was shouting to you and you just stood there! You loosened the rope! You wanted me to fall!' She was shaking with fury and shock and the cold of the rain.

'My dear girl . . .' Morgant began.

'It's true!' Jennie screamed. 'You never wanted me to come! You want Jamie by himself so you can use him to get to the Tower!'

Behind them, Gavan fumbled up the track. Morgant let out his breath slowly. His smile was sickly. 'You're just a little overwrought, my dear,' he said, in a voice that was iron-hard. 'It's understandable. Now I think we should all be roped together, with the two of you in the middle.'

Gavan picked up the ropes.

'No.' Jamie jerked back; his foot sent stones over the edge.

Jennie grabbed him. 'Be careful!'

'Look at them,' he hissed. 'Look at their faces!' Suddenly he lifted his head and shouted at the top of his voice, 'Cai!'

'Silence him!' Morgant snarled, jerking forward.

'Cai!' Jamie yelled. 'You were right!'

A crack of lightning split the sky wide open. For a shocking second they saw each other as white faces; the hot, sulphurous crackle of electricity scorched them, and the ropes in Gavan's hands leapt and jerked. As he held them the ropes shivered and twisted and burst into flame; they were two snakes with tongues and eyes of fire writhing over his chest, and there were others, a nest of them, swarming over the rocks and his legs and wriggling inside Morgant's coat.

Gavan roared and beat at the burning snakes; Jamie tugged Jennie out of her shock. 'Come on!' he yelled, and pushing past Morgant they ran down the wet path, through a maze of rocks, scrambling over scree and bushes, until they swung themselves over into a narrow crack in the rocks and scrambled hastily down.

In the narrow, echoing place at the bottom, their breathing sounded like a crowd of runners. They squatted against the wet stone and let the sound fade, gradually. Far in the distance thunder rumbled.

'Did you see?' Jennie whispered at last. 'Those ropes . . . ?'

The rattle of stones made her stop. They pressed themselves into the darkness. Someone was following; they could see him, scrambling down the cliffside like a black spider, stealthily, with only the tiniest trickles of sound. He dropped lightly to his feet and stood in front of them. Pressed into the shadows, they made no sound, and Jamie thought they were unseen, until the man spoke.

'I wondered when you'd come to your senses.'

Jamie knew the voice. He felt Jennie's hand tighten on his arm but he stepped out, and she followed.

'About time,' Cai said.

'Oh, I know, I know!' Jamie squirmed in self-disgust. 'It's all my fault. I was wrong all the time, trusting those two . . .'

'And now you trust me, I suppose?'

Jamie didn't answer.

'You turned those ropes into snakes, didn't you?' Jennie whispered.

A glimmer of lightning showed them his sharp grin. 'Yes. Not a very – '

He glanced up, then flattened himself instantly against the cliff. Far above them on the path they heard footsteps slithering and ringing on the rocks, and then voices, in a bitter, hissed argument. Slowly the sounds moved away, echoing in crevices. When they were gone, Cai moved. 'In here,' he whispered.

The ravine narrowed, and as they groped their way into it it became a long thin cave, running back into the cliff. Inside, it was black, and damp at first, then turned and twisted back until the walls were dry and they could no longer see the dim entrance.

'Right. This will do,' Cai's voice said.

Around them, the cave began to brighten. They saw him crouching with his hands spread out, and under his fingers a glow, a flicker of flame and sparks, and there was the fire; logs blazing and crackling and roaring out heat without so much as a wisp of smoke. Jamie noticed the long red scar across the man's knuckles. Jennie looked at him, raising her eyebrows; he shrugged, and crouched beside her. The heat rubbed like a cat against their numb fingers and faces, till they tingled and glowed.

Cai sat back lazily against a rock and watched them, his knees bent up like a grasshopper's. 'Have you got anything to eat, vixen?' he asked.

Jennie went red, and shook her head. 'We've eaten it.'

'That's a pity.' He pulled a face. 'Well, first of all, we'll stay here for tonight. The cliff paths are too dangerous in the dark. Then tomorrow we'll have to try and get to the Tower before them.' He stopped, seeing the look on Jamie's face. 'What's the matter with you?'

Jamie folded his arms around his knees and laid his head on them in desperation. 'It's not that easy. They've got the Book. They took it off me.'

Cai stared at him in horror for a moment, tore a hand through his hair, then leapt up and stormed round the cave. 'Nothing but trouble from start to finish!' he snarled. 'Why didn't you trust me from the beginning, you little idiot? I could tear you limb from limb!'

'I'm sorry,' Jamie snapped, 'but it wasn't my fault. They told me things . . . and you scared me.'

'Scared you? How could I have scared you?'

'Well, you're doing a good job now,' Jennie muttered.

The fire flared up and danced on Cai's sharp face; he sank down with a groan and ran his fingers through his hair. 'I suppose they didn't tell much more than the truth,' he said, after a while. 'Most of the things they probably said about me are true – Morgant is clever. But the Book! We need it, and they need you.'

'To get to the Tower?'

'And after. You want to get home, don't you?'

Jamie took his wet coat off and felt the warmth invade him. In that case they'd have to get it back. He didn't fancy waiting a thousand years or so for the next eclipse.

Cai was brooding, huddled up over the fire. Jennie said, 'Well, let's steal it back. Right now, when they don't expect it. It's dark, and Morgant's got a lantern. They'd be easy to find.'

Cai stared into the flames. 'It's too risky. The cliffs

are wet and full of broken rock. They'd hear you coming.'

'But not you, eh?'

He looked up suddenly and grinned at her. 'Don't worry. Tomorrow we'll try it. Dealing with Morgant and his charming assistant would give me a great deal of pleasure.'

Warm through, Jamie arranged his coat around his shoulders and leaned back against a large rock. The cave roof was low and smooth, and in the firelight the floor beneath them felt dry and sandy. The echo of their voices murmured away into quiet; somewhere a drop of water plopped into a pool. He felt comfortable, and glad they would not be moving for a while. Stretching out his legs he said, 'Tell us about the Book. I mean, where it comes from. I don't know anything about it.' A slight tinge of longing for it came to him, and he wished he could feel its smooth black cover under his hand.

'You wouldn't.' Cai spread his long fingers over the fire, and it roared up to lick them. 'No one knows very much about Hu Gadarn's Book.'

'Hu the Strong?'

'That's right. Long ago, they say, he brought his people from the land called the Summer Country, and taught them how to plough the land, how to grow crops and make songs. Some say he was a giant, or that he is immortal. He sailed away in a ship of glass, and no one knows where he went, but he left behind him a book that would tell its guardian the way to the Summer Country. The book is your Book; this is that country.'

'It's not very summery,' Jennie remarked.

'No, and there's a reason. But the Book appears each time the way to this world is open. How it chooses its guardian is a mystery. But it will only answer to you.'

Jamie frowned. 'So Gavan and Morgant . . .'

'Will get nothing. Or,' Cai laughed, 'curses.'

Jennie giggled. 'I can just imagine the Book writing PUSH OFF in nice big capitals.'

'Do they really want to rescue Gweir?' Jamie asked quietly.

Cai's smile faded. 'No. But I do.'

'He's not Morgant's brother, then?'

Cai snorted. 'Is that what he told you? Of course not. The cunning old liar! Morgant has no interest in Gweir. But we have to rescue him. In a way, it's my fault he's a prisoner at all.' He stirred and gazed ruefully into the fire. 'I'm sorry to have to tell you both, but I've been to Fintan's Tower before. And the last time I came I had the same reason as Morgant has now. I came to steal the Cauldron.'

10
Theft

Jamie let out his breath and glanced at Jennie. 'I knew it was that.'

'I think you should explain,' Jennie said. 'You can't ask us to trust you until we know everything. What is this Cauldron, anyway? Why is it so important?'

'Ah, the Cauldron of the King.' Cai leaned back. 'Hasn't the Book told you . . . or perhaps Morgant wouldn't let it?'

He mused for a moment, his face a web of red light and leaping shadows. Then he said, 'The Cauldron of the King of Annwn is kept guarded in Fintan's Tower, by the Nine Maidens. It is kept safe because it is a hallowed thing; it has many powers, but most important among them is that it can give knowledge. If the Cauldron is filled with certain herbs and elixirs and kept boiling for a year and a day, whoever drinks of the liquid within it will have all knowledge and all power. You can see why Morgant wants it – and why we can't let him have it.'

'Yes.' Jamie was thoughtful. 'Yes, I can.'

'Well, many years ago, the Emperor heard of the Cauldron's power; he decided to try and get it for himself. We fitted out an expedition of three ship-loads of men, and sailed here, at a time when the way was open.'

'Sailed?' Jennie interrupted. 'From where?'

Cai frowned. 'Logria. Don't interrupt. Morgant

advised the Emperor that it was a good thing to do; I'm afraid to say I agreed. Some of the others didn't, even then.'

'And what happened?'

Cai shrugged, as if he disliked remembering. 'The whole thing was a disaster. Three shiploads came, and only seven men went back; I was lucky to be one. Unfortunately Morgant was another. As for the others, they were lost, or killed as we fought our way out. It was a nightmare; Fintan's Tower is a maze of sorceries, of corridors and strange chambers. Nothing can be trusted there – even my memory of it is confused . . .' He shivered, as if trying to shake something off. 'We fought against wraiths and shadows. And Gweir, of all of us – Gweir, whom I was supposed to look after – was captured. I'm not sure how; some said afterwards that he reached the Cauldron and touched it, and melted into air. Since then his cries have echoed through the land of Summer. Once, wherever he walked flowers sprang up, birds sang, the weather was warm. Since he has been in Fintan's Tower the Summer Country has mourned for him, as you see it now.'

Jamie thought of the black, twisted trees, the empty grass.

'This Emperor,' Jennie said slowly. 'Where is his court?'

'I told you. Logria. The Island of the Mighty.'

'But that's an old name for Britain.'

'Yes.' Cai looked at her sideways. 'Britain is Logria. The land of the real can also be the land of the unreal. As one coin can have two sides, each different. Logria is the underside of Britain.'

'But . . .'

Cai held up his hand. 'That's enough. No more

questions. Time is getting on and you should sleep.'
And as he refused to answer anything more, they had
to make the best of it. Wishing he was not so hungry,
Jamie settled himself on the sandy floor, tried to make
a pillow of the rucksack, turned and squirmed to get
himself comfortable. And while he was still listening
to Cai's and Jennie's voices, and thinking he would
never fall asleep, he fell asleep.

Breakfast is a difficult thing to do without. 'Hot por-
ridge,' Jamie muttered. 'Piping hot in a blue bowl.'

'Toast, dripping with butter.'

'Bacon and eggs.'

'Oh stop it!' Jennie said crossly. 'It only makes
things worse.'

Jamie stopped rubbing his arms, and staggered to
his feet. 'I'm stiff too. My legs feel as if they're bruised
all over.'

The fire was out, and there was no sign of where it
had been. Cai was coming back down the cave, his
footsteps noiseless on the sand.

'I've found them,' he said, squatting down. 'It
wasn't hard – our friend Gavan leaves a trail like a
herd of horses. And they're still asleep . . .'

'I wish I was,' Jennie muttered.

'. . . which will make it easier for us. Come on,
and listen now, Jamie.' Cai caught his arm irritably.
'Remember, they want you as much as we want the
Book. If you think you are in danger – vanish. Forget
honour, forget me, even forget the vixen here. Just
go!'

He nodded, but caught Jennie looking at him. 'He
won't,' she said. 'Just you watch.'

As they came out of the cave the sky was still dark,
with a faint greyness tingeing it. The stars were fading,

and the intense cold of the air made them shudder. Silently, Cai led them up to the cliff path, and along it for about ten minutes, often walking warily ahead to make sure it was safe. In the early dawn nothing moved but themselves. The rocks were frosty and slippery underfoot. They could barely see the country they were coming down to; a thick white fog clung to it, masking all but the tops of a few hills. As they went down into it, the air grew damp and thick about them, and their breath smoked.

When they left the path they seemed to have come almost to the bottom of the cliffs. The undergrowth here was thick and tangled; black brambles and thorns were coated with a spiky fur of frost. Quietly, they shouldered through. Cai stretched out and bent back a bough; then he motioned them forward. They saw the red glow of a fire; a little way from it Gavan was sitting, his back against a tree, his legs stretched out in front of him. He was snoring gently. Morgant was a dark huddle by the fire; his knees were drawn up under his coat and they could see the corner of the canvas bag poking out. His left arm was tight around it.

'The Book's in there,' Jamie whispered to Cai.

The tall man nodded. Then he pushed them back a little way and crouched down. 'Here's what we do. I'm going to see to Gavan. When I've finished, you and I, Jennie, will try to get the Book. *If* we're lucky we might get it without waking them. If we separate, meet in that little copse down there.' He nodded over Jamie's shoulder. 'See it?'

'Yes, but –'

'But nothing.' With a swish of branches he was gone.

Jamie and Jennie waited, trying not to make a

sound. They were so cold that they wanted to shift about, and Jamie's right foot began to go to sleep. Then they saw him.

He had worked his way round to the opposite side of the clearing; his dark shape flickered through the mist until he stood behind Gavan's tree. Jamie stiffened. From the greyness behind the tree a rope of fine silvery stuff was sliding out, slithering along the ground. It wound over Gavan's sprawled legs, ran over his body and slid around the tree trunk. Round and round the rope moved, over his shoulders, under his arms, cocooning him in its soft, silent web. Once he shifted, sleepily, but the rope ran gently around his neck and went back to Cai.

When it was finished, Cai crept stealthily back.

'Now, vixen. You try to get the Book. If Morgant wakes, leave him to me. You just grab the bag and go.'

She grinned at Jamie, and shoved the rucksack at him.

'Good luck.' He watched them through the drifts of mist; they emerged quietly from the bushes and Cai squatted by Morgant.

Jennie went round him, and got down on her hands and knees. Jamie could see how still and white she was. She went a little closer, until she was crouching by Morgant's side; if he had opened his eyes he would have seen her. Carefully, she reached towards the bag, caught hold of a corner of it, and tugged, ever so slightly. Jamie held his breath. Morgant did not stir, but the bag would not come; even in his sleep he held it tight. She glanced at Cai, who made a signal in the air with his hand; Jamie saw her nod, and begin, infinitely slowly, to undo one of the straps. It was impossible! She'd never get it out! He was holding his breath; around him the land was silent. Only the wind rustled the branches and lifted the ends of Jennie's hair as she inched the leather tongue from the buckle and a dark hole showed itself in the canvas. Gently, oh so gently, she slid her hand inside.

And Morgant moved! Before Jamie could yell a warning the old man was up and shouting to Gavan; he held Jennie tight and Cai was sprawling in the bushes as if he had been hurled aside. Gavan shuddered and woke; he tried to leap up, but the ropes held him. He scrabbled and tore at them furiously. Jamie watched Cai pick himself up painfully and rush at Morgant, but the moment he touched the old man, Morgant snatched up a branch and flung it; as it brushed Cai's shoulder it burst into flames. The clearing was a confusion of noise and mist and sudden smoke; Gavan roared and fought with the shining ropes. Jamie saw one snap, then another; then Cai dragged Jennie away and they were running, crashing through the bushes.

'Get after them!' Morgant screamed, his voice raw with anger, and with a mighty, snapping heave Gavan was on his feet and gone. In the silence that remained, Morgant turned. He was breathing hard. His small black eyes gazed coldly into the bushes.

'And you, Jamie,' he said quietly. 'Where are you?'

Ice-cold, Jamie held himself still. Morgant came nearer; Jamie forced himself not to move. He could outrun him, but it would be too easy to get himself lost. Morgant waited, a small grey man in the dawn. Then he said, 'You're quiet, but I can hear you. I can hear your breath, I can hear the creaking of your boots. I can hear the blood in your veins and the air in your nostrils. I am Morgant, Jamie. I left Logria to seek power, and I have it. Come out, Jamie.'

Despairing, Jamie bit his lip. And then a voice behind him answered his prayer.

'You can't hear anyone but me, friend.'

And the small brown man with the donkey brushed past him and strode into the clearing.

11

The Man from Yesterday

Morgant was as surprised as Jamie. He glared at the stranger. 'You again? Where did you come from? Are you following us?'

The small man smiled and patted the donkey's neck. 'Our paths certainly seem fated to cross. Were you looking for someone else?'

Morgant frowned into the bushes, then turned away. 'I suppose I was mistaken.' He stopped, and shot a swift glance at the man over his shoulder. 'I thought this country was empty. Are you one of the people of the Tower?'

The infuriating smile did not waver. 'This is my country.' The man rubbed the donkey's ears and it nuzzled him. 'As far as it is anyone's, that is.' But as Morgant turned in disgust to follow Gavan, the stranger said, 'One thing, friend.'

Morgant stopped, but did not turn.

'Fintan's Tower is a centre of great peril. Its treasures are forbidden. I think I should warn you . . .'

'Warn me!' Morgant snapped.

'. . . to go back where you came from, and to cease to feed this hunger that torments you. What use is knowledge, if you do not have wisdom?'

For a second Morgant turned his head. He looked puzzled, almost shaken.

'Who are you?' he asked.

The stranger smiled. 'Your conscience,' he said.

77

For half a moment Morgant stood. Then he pushed into the frosty bushes and Jamie heard him rustling away.

Slowly, Jamie stood up and brushed the white melting ice from his knees and hair. The small man watched him. 'Come,' he said. 'Let's find your friends.'

'Why didn't you give me away?'

The man laughed. 'Come on. This way.'

The copse that Cai had pointed out was not far, but they went along the base of the cliffs first, and round in a wide circle before they approached it. Under the branches were deep drifts of crisp, golden leaves up to Jamie's ankles, but between the aisles of trees the place seemed deserted.

'Jennie?' he murmured. 'It's all right.'

A noise behind made him turn; he saw Jennie's legs slither through the branches, then she dropped down lightly and grinned at him. Morgant's bag came down with a thud, and then Cai. They looked at the stranger warily.

'You're the man from yesterday,' Jennie said. 'We asked you the way.'

'That's right.' He sat himself down comfortably on a fallen trunk and smiled at her. 'I didn't like the look of what I saw; I thought it would be wise to keep an eye on things. Just as well, wouldn't you say?'

Cai scowled. 'Did you see me too?'

'No, I didn't, and that makes you quite remarkable.' The man waved his arm. 'But I know who you are. Cai the Cantankerous. Cai the Fair. Arthur's brother.'

Jamie thought that would make him angry, but Cai just grinned. 'And your name?'

'Doesn't matter. Have you got what you wanted?'

Already Jennie had Morgant's bag open, and now she pulled out the Book. 'Yes. It's this.'

She handed it up to Jamie, who opened it.

Hello, the Book wrote amiably.

'Hello,' Jamie said, a strange warm relief filling him. 'Are you all right?'

Quite, thank you.

'And guess what.' Jennie looked up at them hesitantly. 'There's food in here.'

'Let's have it,' Cai said at once.

She pulled out a small cheese wrapped in cloth, and some bread and apples. Cai picked up one of the apples and bit into it. 'Go on. You're hungry.'

'But it's stealing.' For some reason Jennie looked at the stranger. 'Isn't it?'

'I don't care,' Jamie said, squatting down to the bread and cheese. 'They stole the Book; they deserve it. Anyway, we can always leave them some, if you're that fussy.'

But in the end there was not much to leave; once they started eating they found out just how hungry they were. Guiltily, Jennie hung the almost empty bag on the branch of a tree. 'They'll find it,' Cai said grimly. 'Morgant has ways.'

The stranger ate nothing, but watched them, smiling and chewing his blade of grass. When they were ready to go he said, 'Now I'll come with you for a while. I know where the Tower is, and I know that every step of the way you will be in danger. The man Morgant has a hunger in him for glory; he has an evil smile. The other one is a roaring furnace. Watch your backs, my friends.'

He led them out of the copse and down a narrow

track that ran through scattered woodland and gorse. The mist had lifted by now, but the sky kept its usual coppery tinge. Jamie found himself wishing for the sun, and glancing at his watch he found nearly half a minute had passed. He tried to think of the astronomers on the hill top moving infinitely slowly, as if in some slowed-down film, but it was too bizarre. There was no sign of any pursuit but, as Cai said, the trail of four people and a donkey was one even Gavan could find. They moved swiftly, carrying nothing with them but the Book, in its rucksack.

The stranger led his donkey in front, rubbing its neck and chatting to Jennie, who walked beside him. Jamie heard her ask him the donkey's name. Behind them came Cai, wrapped up in his dark coat and unusually thoughtful.

They walked a long way, down small valleys and up again to bleak hilltops, through a wood where the trees were all interlaced above their heads, down a path beside a river that roared and foamed over stones and jutting rocks. And still the land was silent, with no birds, no fish, not even an insect on the path; just the faint murmur of the wind and the drip of melting frost.

Just as Jamie was getting tired, they came to a place where the river plunged over a waterfall, and the path, too, ran steeply down.

They sat down to rest in the trees, and Jamie took the chance to ask Cai, 'How do we know he's taking us the right way?'

'Don't you trust him?' Cai asked lazily.

'Well, yes. I mean, he didn't tell Morgant I was there . . .'

'So don't worry.' Cai watched the stranger's small

greeny-brown figure approach through the trees. 'The Tower is nearer than you think.'

The small man came and crouched beside them. 'It is time,' he said, 'that we spoke with the Ancients of the world.'

Cai shrugged. 'There's no need . . .'

'Still. We should let them see what time is, and what wisdom is.' He took the Book from Jamie's bag and held it open, and with a shrug and a movement of his hands Cai lit a fire which crackled before the spread pages. Jamie felt Jennie crouch next to him.

'Time,' said the stranger, 'is mystery. A moment may be eternity; eternity a moment. Look.'

On the page was a bird, small and black. It stepped out of the Book into the flickering flames.

'Speak of the Prisoner,' Cai said softly. 'Arthur's messengers seek him.'

'I am old,' the bird said. 'I have sharpened my beak on the anvil every evening, until now it is as small as a walnut. I have not heard of this Prisoner. But there are those older than I.'

On the next page was a stag, grazing. It took a mouthful of flames from the fire and chewed them thoughtfully. 'I am old,' the stag said. 'I have known a sapling grow to an oak with a hundred branches and dwindle to a red stump. In all that time I have not heard of the Prisoner you seek. But there are those older than I.'

Silently, the stranger turned the page. An owl grew to huge size, preened one feather into the flames. 'I am old,' the owl said. 'I have seen three forests rise and fall in this same valley. I have not heard of the man you seek. There are others, however, older than I.'

Cai nodded, the owl flickered into darkness. An

81

eagle glared out at them through the smoke and flames.

'Speak of Gweir,' Cai whispered. 'Arthur's messenger seeks.'

'I am old,' the eagle said. 'I have pecked at the stars from a mountain top, and time has worn it away till it is not a handsbreadth high. I know nothing of him. But there is one older even than I.'

Almost fearfully, Jamie saw the page turn. With a flick of its tail a salmon swam out into the heat and smoke. 'Listen,' it said. 'Once as I swam by the walls of the fortress in the lake, I heard wailing and lamenting on the far side of the wall. It was a man in sorrow. Seek your Prisoner in the Fortress of Glass.'

The pages were empty; the fire crackled.

Slowly, the stranger closed the Book.

Jamie sat back with a sigh. 'It's amazing,' Jennie breathed, chin on fists. 'I'm not even sure I heard those things – were they written or did I hear them?'

The small man shrugged and gave the Book back to Jamie. 'Who knows.' Jamie had opened the Book. On the page was written:

Fintan's Tower is before you.

'What do you mean?'

Stand up, it wrote, *and look*.

So he did.

Through the trees he saw soft, spreading countryside, and beyond it the peaks of distant mountains. Something glittered through the trees. He went forward a little, shouldered through the low branches of conifers, then reached out and pulled the greenery gently aside.

In front of him was a great lake, its surface clear and rippled, reflecting the sky. And out on the water, as if it floated there in the rising mists, he saw a tower, curiously shaped, gleaming with a pale, greenish light. The mist from the lake drifted across it; he caught glimpses of dark windows, and a great door lit with torches, and one light, high up near the battlements, where the tower sprouted turrets and balconies and staircases. There it was, as he had seen it in the ring of fire that day in the farm kitchen. Fintan's Tower.

Jennie had followed him.

'It's huge,' he said.

'Yes.' She gazed out at the lake. 'Jamie, have you thought about what will happen when we get there? What's going to stop us ending up prisoners ourselves?'

With a sigh Jamie let the branches swing back into place. 'Don't ask me. The future, you might say, is a blank.'

When they came down from the trees the path grew wider and firmer, until it was a great road running down in a long curve to the shores of the lake. As they trudged along it, afternoon turned slowly into evening, and Jamie felt his hunger come creeping back. He hitched the bag up on his shoulders and glanced behind. No sign of pursuit. They had travelled quickly.

'Not long now,' the small man said, and as Jamie turned he saw that they had nearly reached the water, and that the road ended abruptly at the lake's edge, among sedges and black, broken reeds.

'How do we cross?' he muttered to Cai.

Cai shrugged. 'Boat.'

'But what if there isn't . . . ?'

'There will be.'

And there was. Jennie tugged a rope hanging in the water and pulled it into sight; a small, slimy-looking wooden boat, with a strange high prow. There were no oars.

The small man ruffled the donkey's ears. 'Goodbye,' he said. 'And good luck.'

They stared at him. 'Aren't you coming?' Jamie asked.

'No. This is your business – and yours,' he added, glancing up at Cai. 'Not mine.' He took the Book from its bag under Jamie's arm and opened it. 'What do you think?'

Your place is elsewhere, the Book wrote, to Jamie's astonishment. *I will look after them, as far as the enchantments of the Tower allow.*

'Good,' the stranger said. 'I leave it with you then, for the moment.' And he turned the donkey's head and began to lead it slowly back up the road. 'Be careful. Look ahead and look behind, and above all, look within.'

'Goodbye,' Jamie said sadly, and Jennie echoed him.

'I'll tell the Court I saw you,' Cai said.

They saw the man was laughing; he waved his arm but did not turn around.

'What do you mean?' Jennie asked. 'Do you know who he is?'

'The Book answered him.' And Cai nodded down at the words that Jamie was already reading on the white page.

Goodbye, Hu Gadarn, the Book had written.

12
Fortress of Frustration

'Careful!' The boat swung round perilously as Jennie stepped in; she sat down hastily.

Jamie came last, grabbing Cai's cold hand as he stumbled.

'Good,' Cai said, and leaned back, easing out his long legs.

'Yes, but how do we row? There aren't any oars.'

Cai grinned. 'We don't need them.' As he said it, the boat began to move. It turned slowly, so that the prow faced out across the misty lake, and then, as if it was carried in a strong current, or pushed by invisible hands, it moved out over the water.

The silence was uncanny, broken only by the soft sound of ripples under the prow. In the growing gloom the lake smelt of weeds, and dank, rotting vegetation; the water was dim with shadows and icy to the touch, and when Jamie leaned over the side he saw only his own reflection swaying on the surface, and the impossibly large crescent of the moon above him. Slowly, the lakeside fell away behind them.

Looking back, Jennie said, 'Is that Hu, there by that tree?'

A shadow flickered among the bushes at the edge of the lake. Someone was looking after them.

Cai scowled. 'I doubt it,' he said.

Suddenly the mist was around them. White and faintly glistening, it was damp against their faces; it left chill drops on their clothes and the wooden boards of the boat. Everything became blurred, difficult to see, and when they spoke their voices sounded louder than usual, so that they almost whispered. Slowly, the boat drifted into whiteness that sometimes opened to give glimpses of dark water or a sky full of stars, and then closed over them again, with its frosty, moon-white web.

Gradually, they began to hear water lapping not far ahead; the boat seemed to drift more slowly. Kneeling up, Jamie stared ahead into the mist; it shimmered and drifted apart, and for a second he saw clear water, and the mighty bulk of a wall reflected high over him.

'Look!' he gasped, but they were already staring up at it; the battlements and turrets and smooth embrasures that seemed to lean out over their heads. Silent and far up on the topmost pinnacle, a man leaned over and watched them. Then the mist closed in, and the tower was lost.

'Someone saw us,' Jennie whispered.

'Sentinel,' Cai muttered. He seemed uneasy. 'It happened before.' Then the boat bumped against something hard, and stopped.

Carefully, Cai manoeuvred himself over the side; he dragged the slimy rope from the water and looped it round a jutting crag of what seemed like ice. Jamie clambered out after him, and Jennie followed, handing out the bag.

They found themselves standing on a slippery, jagged surface. In front of them, so close they could touch it, a great wall rose up into the mists, made of some smooth-looking greenish substance. Jamie took his glove off and felt the surface; it was smooth, with seams and bubbles of air trapped inside, icy to touch, with that echo of green light. It was made of great blocks fitted tightly together with no gaps between.

'It feels like glass,' he muttered. 'A tower of glass.'

And they walked on glass, smooth in places, in others jagged and broken, its edges wickedly sharp. Careful not to slip and cut themselves, they followed Cai along the base of the enormous wall.

Soon they came to steps cut from the glass, and climbed up them. Great torches flared on each side as they came under the shadow of the walls. The door, when they reached it, was equally huge, but wooden and bound with great bronze hinges. It was locked, but the key stood in the keyhole.

'Now look,' Cai said, turning. 'I don't know what will be waiting for us in here. We have been seen; that was only to be expected. Expect anything; be ready for anything. And don't forget those other two charmers are behind us. Keep close, don't wander off, above all, guard the Book.' He paused, and looked at Jamie narrowly. 'I suppose you won't let me take care of it?'

'Sorry, no.' Jamie gripped the straps of the rucksack. 'I think it would rather be with me.'

Jennie giggled. 'You make it sound as if it's alive.'

'I think it is.'

Still, they made him go in the middle, and Jennie came last, although Jamie knew she was nervous about things coming up behind her. When they were ready, Cai turned the key and pushed open the door.

It moved slowly and heavily, with a low rumble; he shoved it wide, and as it banged against the wall they crowded behind him to look in. The corridor in front of them was dim and draughty. Tiny swirls of dust and ice stirred over the floor.

'Looks empty.' Jamie's whisper echoed down the walls.

Cai stepped inside, and peered ahead. 'We're not that lucky. Come on, and leave the door open. We may want to get out in a hurry.'

There was a faint greenish light in the passageway, as if moonlight was filtering in through the thick slabs of glass, but as they crept further in it faded to a glimmer, until Jamie could just see Cai as a blackness moving in front of him. When it became too dark to see at all, they stopped. The rustles and whispers of their progress died away, and everything was utterly silent. Fintan's Tower gave no sign of life.

'I'm going to try a light,' Cai's voice said, after a moment. 'Get ready.'

For a second nothing happened. Then a small ball of fire grew in the darkness; its own light showed them it was balanced at the tips of his fingers. With a sharp flick he sent it wobbling through the air in front of them, its glow lighting the passage a pale unsteady yellow. They saw a smooth floor and walls turning a corner not far ahead. Cai walked on stealthily, his feet making no sound on the slippery floor, and Jamie followed, trying to be as quiet. At the corner, Cai sent the light round first, then, waving at them to keep back, peered after it.

Then he tore his hand through his hair and groaned.

Jamie pushed him aside and looked. It was a crossroads. In each direction a passage led away, as dark and cold and damp as the one they were in. Each disappeared round a corner. Each was identical, and silent.

'It's a maze,' Jennie muttered over his shoulder. 'Look, shouldn't we try to mark our way, or something? Otherwise we'll never be able to get back out.'

'String, you mean,' Jamie said.

'Or breadcrumbs, if we had any.'

'Quiet!' Cai snapped. The ball hovering over his shoulder crackled and spat; his cold fingers twitched the bag from Jamie's shoulder. 'Ask that!'

Grinning at Jennie, Jamie opened the Book. 'Can you tell us the way?'

To his astonishment the page turned black. If there was any writing, he couldn't see it. He turned the page and asked again, and then again, but each page was black and useless. Cai snatched it from him and riffled through it, then threw it back in disgust.

'What use is that!' he stormed, quietly. 'Just when we need it!'

'What's wrong with it?'

'The Guardians have silenced it!'

'Or perhaps it's just asleep,' Jamie said, to hide his worry.

'Idiot. Perhaps it will wear off,' Jennie suggested. 'Anyway, I don't think you should lose your temper over it.'

With a withering look, Cai marched off into the left-hand tunnel, hurtling the globe of light through the air in front of him.

Jennie pushed Jamie after him. 'He's just picked this one at random. It won't be long before we're lost in here.'

It soon seemed to Jamie that she was right. The passageways became an endless labyrinth and they just seemed to be going deeper and deeper and getting more confused. They passed turnings, tried a left one, then a right one, went down corridors to blank walls and then came back; but nowhere were there any doors, or rooms, or windows, or, most important, stairs.

'It's the stairs we need to find,' Cai muttered, as they paused for breath in the centre of a web of openings. 'We need to climb up, probably to the top, where the light is. It's where Gweir will be.'

'But surely,' Jennie objected, 'he'd be in a dungeon, or something.'

Cai snorted, and Jamie said quickly, 'It's a tower, Jen. The safest place would be at the top.'

'All right, clever. And he won't be guarded, I suppose?'

'He'd better be,' Cai said grimly. 'I'm just in the mood to deal with them.'

It must have been five minutes after that that they heard the noise: a great clap of sound rumbling in the air, and a vibration that seemed to shake the solid glass slabs underfoot.

'What was that?' Jennie grabbed at Jamie's arm.

'Ow!'

'Sshh!'

Stiff with dread, they let the rumbles die away into silence. When they were quite gone, Cai still waited, listening. Finally, he walked on.

'Well, what was it?' Jennie asked.

'I think,' he said quietly, 'that it was the door. Someone closed it.'

It had to have been Morgant and Gavan, Jamie was still convinced five minutes later. That meant they were in here too, going round in this maze, like mice in a laboratory. Maybe even round the next corner their shadows would be lurking . . . the small shadow of Morgant and the grey hulk that would be Gavan. And if not them, the Guardians Cai seemed so wary of. The people of the Tower – who were they? Who was Fintan? It occurred to him that they should have asked the Book a lot more questions, and now it was too late and they were in trouble.

Cai obviously thought so too. He had fiercely forbidden talking, and had moved a few metres ahead, edging up to every corner and listening cautiously. The cold seemed to be getting worse; the glass was like ice; their breath began to float about them. We're getting deeper and deeper, Jamie thought. Colder and colder. The walls were blue and green, bubbled and seamed, translucent thick ice. He paused and put his face close to them, brushing away the frost of his breath. Surely there were things trapped deep in there, like flies in amber. Surely he could see hands and faces, the curve of fingers round a sword hilt, the paws of some beast? As he moved, the images twisted and blurred, grew and shrank; he thought he saw the frozen pelt of a wolf, its mouth open in a snarl.

Jennie thudded into his stillness.

'What's the matter?' she whispered.

He shook his head and pulled her on, thinking of the lost men of the Emperor's expedition. They had come with force and met it, it seemed. He began to be afraid of Fintan's silent Tower.

Cai was waiting for them. He caught Jamie's arm. 'Look,' he breathed.

Ahead, the corridor ran smoothly, and at the far end of it was a door: a large, strong wooden door, with metal hinges and a key in the keyhole. The globe of light bumped against it gently and bounced back, like a bubble.

'Oh no,' Jennie muttered. 'It's the way we came in. We've been going round in circles.'

'Rubbish,' Cai said sharply. 'This is what we've been looking for all along!'

13

Fortress of Carousal

Pressed flat against the wall, feeling its damp chill through his coat, Jamie watched the dark slot of the door.

Jennie's breath tickled his ear. 'He's been gone ages.'

'A few minutes. Less.'

'Perhaps they've got him.'

'Him? I pity them!'

A shuffle in the doorway froze them; then Cai's tall shape blocked the gap. 'All right,' he said. 'But keep very quiet.'

He moved aside to let them through, then closed the door with a soft click.

Jamie stared before him in surprise. The globe of white fire still hung in the air, but the room had its own light. A long wooden table ran down the centre, and on each corner of it was a candlestick with seven slim candles, their wax guttering into grotesque shapes and dripping in pools on the polished wood. The table was loaded with food: dishes of apples, great haunches of meat, steaming fish, hot stews and bread, strange fruits and sweetmeats. The mingled smell of herbs and ginger and lemon drifted around them.

'Is all that real?' Jamie whispered, after a while.

'Oh yes,' Cai said. 'Real enough. It depends what you mean by real. Are you real?'

Jamie glanced at Jennie, and grinned. 'Of course I'm real.' He went over and picked up a soft red strawberry and sniffed it. 'Smells great. Can we eat it?'

'No!'

'I knew you'd say that.'

Cai crossed the room, snatched the fruit away and flung it down. 'Leave it. It's here to delay us, or ensnare us, or worse. I've seen what would happen if you ate it, and it isn't pleasant. Now this is far more important.'

He pushed them hurriedly towards the corner of the room, and through a small arch they saw a tiny thread of stairway that led up, twisting tightly round on itself.

'This is it. Now keep close. There's no way of knowing what's up here. You, vixen, keep your eyes open for anything behind you.'

She pulled a face at Jamie, but he saw she was worried. 'I'll go last, Jen, if you want.'

'No you won't.' Cai tugged him back. 'You'll go in the middle and keep quiet. She'll be all right. She . . .' He stopped, his gaze fixing over their shoulders.

The candles were out. The table was white with dust and cobwebs – thick, hanging webs, centuries old. The food – if you could still call it that – was a brown sticky mess on the plates.

'*Yuk*,' Jamie said, too loudly.

Cai grabbed him; it was too late. The echoes rippled round the room; rang above their heads in the spiral tunnel of the stairs. And at once, somewhere far off in the depths of the Tower, they heard a sudden snatch of noise – voices, music, laughter – cut off at once as if an undiscovered door had opened and closed again. And in the stillness that followed, their ears slowly caught it, a new sound, a soft padding and snuffling out there in the labyrinth of corridors, and then, echoing round the miles of twists and corners and passageways, a long, eerie howl, as if some creature like a dog had been locked out in the dark.

For a moment none of them spoke. The sound chilled their spines and fingers. Then Jennie said, 'They've let something loose. It's looking for us.'

Cai whipped around. 'Change of plan. I'll go last – Jennie to the front. Move!'

They raced up the stairs, slowing a little as they lost breath. Like the walls, the steps were glass, damp and slithery, climbing steeply. Cai, who seemed not to get breathless at all, urged them to hurry.

'I am!' Jamie gasped. His chest ached, and the Book banged heavily about in its rucksack and bruised his shoulders.

The higher they climbed, the colder the air; touching the walls froze their fingers. Then Jennie stopped dead.

'Empty space!' she hissed back.

Cai jerked to listen behind him. 'Go on, but carefully!'

They crowded to the top step and looked into the emptiness. It was a great dark hall, enormous and deserted. High up on one side were tall windows; through them they could see the occasional glimmer of the moon through clouds. A cold wind blew in. The globe hung over their heads, a tiny spark of light in a cold echoing place.

Without a word, Jennie began to walk forward, her quiet footsteps crunching the frost on the floor. They followed her, one at each side, eyes alert for any movement in the shadows; the moon, travelling through the clouds outside, slid a long wand of light across the hall and stretched shadows behind them.

At the far end was a dim structure; they walked swiftly towards it. As they came close, Jamie thought he saw something move, and stopped with a hissed warning. After a moment they went on. By now the globe of light had drifted ahead of them; it showed three shallow steps of green bubbled glass, and as it rose over the steps, magically there were globes of light everywhere, hanging in the air, each identical and moving as one.

Cai looked astonished. For a moment Jamie was too bewildered to understand. Then he realized.

'Mirrors!'

Around the platform the glass walls were polished in places to a gleaming sharpness. As Jennie walked up the steps, she flashed into the mirrors; nine Jennies, identically dirty and dishevelled, glimmered in the shadows and half-darkness. And in the ninefold light of the globe they saw what the great, round dark thing in the centre was: an enormous cauldron, made of some heavy, dark-blue metal, chased and patterned all over with thin gold lines whirling and twisting so the eye couldn't follow them. Around the rim were huge pearls, with strange, stick-like letters carved under them. The whole thing hung from three chains of mighty links, each the size of a hand; the chains ran upwards into the roof and were lost in the darkness, as if they hung from the sky itself.

'So that's what it looks like,' Cai said, almost to himself.

Something in his voice made Jamie turn and look at him. The moonlight caught his hair and it gleamed; his eyes were dark in the shadows of his face.

'You still want it!'

'Want it?' Cai let out his breath in a gasp of laughter. 'Think of knowing everything, Jamie, everything that's been and that's still to come.' The nine globes seemed to sparkle and crackle around him; his long hand grabbed Jamie's shoulder. 'Knowing all wizardry; being such a master of sorcery that in all Logria no one could outwit you. To know yourself. Anyone would want that!'

'I wouldn't.' Jamie squirmed out of his grip and leapt up two of the steps. 'I don't. I don't want to know everything – not all the horrible, dark, wicked things, all the fear and evil. You'd know those too, wouldn't you? Besides, we're not here for the Cauldron, we're here for Gweir – or had you forgotten?'

Cai glared at him furiously. 'Of course I haven't!'

'Well, shut up about the Cauldron. We're not going to steal it.'

'I don't know *how* to steal it,' Cai snapped back. 'Besides, if you touch it . . .' He gasped, jerked round and saw Jennie on the platform. 'Jennie,' he yelled, his voice rising in panic, 'don't touch it! *Don't touch it*!'

Her hand on the dark-blue rim, she stared at him in horror. And as they watched, she faded; her outline shimmered and became a shadow filled with pale smoke that slowly drifted away into the open spaces of the hall and dwindled into nothing.

The platform and the mirrors were empty.

And somewhere below them, in the maze of passages, that long howl sounded nearer.

14

The Prison of Gweir

Cai snapped out of the shock first. He tore the rucksack from Jamie's shoulder, threw it down on the floor
and tugged out the Book.

'Ask it! Ask it quickly!'

Below them the howl came again, and then a
sudden, urgent yelp. 'It's got the scent,' Cai said
grimly.

Jamie jerked the Book open. 'Please tell us where
she is . . . what's happened to her. Please try – it's
coming up the stairs!'

The black page rippled, turned grey, then back to
black, as if it struggled with its own nature. Then tiny
white letters crammed themselves hurriedly together
at the bottom of the page.

*I shouldn't, they have forbidden me, but . . . the other
stairs. In the corner to your right.*

He had barely read them before they blinked out.

'In the corner – over there!'

Cai was already moving; Jamie grabbed the bag and
raced after him. Behind the Cauldron it was dark and
dusty; Cai sent the globe of light spinning ahead of
him.

The staircase was broader than the one they had
come up, but hidden behind a jutting slab of wall.
They threw themselves up, two steps at a time, Jamie

with the Book still gripped tight under his arm. Cai ran quicker; he was soon out of sight round the twisting pillar, his footsteps ringing over Jamie's head. 'Wait!' Jamie gasped. 'Wait for me!'

The footsteps turned; Cai thundered back and hauled him up with one long arm. 'We can't wait!'

'Then go on . . . I'll have to . . . catch breath. Just get Jennie.'

In the silence between his gasps, they heard nothing. Below them the stairs were empty.

'If anything comes, shout.'

'What do you think I'll do . . . dance?'

Cai grinned, thumped him on the head and was gone, sprinting lightly up into the darkness. The globe drifted after him, and blackness closed in.

Jamie sat on the stairs, bent double with the ferocious stitch in his side. He tried to breathe slowly, felt the sweat on his back turning cold. It was quiet; the pattering of Cai's feet was almost lost in the layers of stone over his head. It sounded so far off he was alarmed and stood up to follow, and it was then he heard something else.

Breathing.

It was coming from just below him, somewhere down in the darkness. He stood still, ears straining for the faint sound, his eyes fixed on the wall twisting down out of sight. Yes, there it was – quiet breathing, almost panting, as if some creature was climbing up the steps towards him, in no hurry, but moving easily and stealthily. Now he could catch the pad of its paws, and a few small clicks against the glass. A shadow flickered on the wall.

It was too late to shout. He moved up, walking backwards, step by step, soundlessly. Any minute, it could leap round that bend. After four steps he paused. The stairs were silent.

It hasn't gone, he thought. It's sitting down there, listening, sniffing the air.

His heart pounded – he could hear it. The stairwell was black and empty and nothing moved but a thin cold draught of air that tickled his cheek. He brushed at it, then glanced up.

In the glass wall above his head was a door; infinitely carefully he edged up two more steps and pushed at it. The door opened.

At once the padding began, swift and close. He hauled himself up through the door and closed it with a hurried click, pressing himself against it, gasping in the bitter cold. No wonder – he was outside!

The moon dragged a trail of cloud behind it; the strange stars glittered in a black sky. He was standing on a tiny broken parapet with no edge, and below him – far, far below – the black water lapped at the base of the wall, its surface streaked and silvered with the shifting moonlight.

His breath smoked. Behind him, something flung itself against the door with a thud that jarred him forward; he braced himself in terror and pushed back, arms rigid between the doorposts. If it opened now, it wouldn't matter what came through, he would fall, down and down, to the icy water and splinters of deadly glass. It was snuffling now, scratching and growling under the door. The wind whistled round the corner of the Tower and flapped his coat. In a sudden giddiness, he felt the whole world turning slowly under him; glimpsed the moon in its eerie procession through the torn, silvery clouds.

Then he gripped tight, and looked up.

From somewhere above him in the fortress a light

must be shining; he could see its glimmer stretch far out over the water. And as he stood there, he was sure he could hear someone shouting – no, wailing; wailing and crying out loud as if in some terrible trouble. As the wind shifted, it was gone. Had it been Gweir, lamenting in his prison? Or Jennie, in hers?

Behind him, the door was silent. The creature might have gone by now; in any case he was stiff with cold. He tugged the door open, and then, when nothing leapt at his throat, he slid inside, shivering. The stairs seemed empty. Uneasily, he closed the door and began to climb, and then, not far above him, he heard a low savage growl – a vicious sound. Panic struck him. Suddenly he tore up the steps, round and round, hurtled out into a dark corridor, raced down it, turned the corner and stopped dead.

The corridor was lit with torches, red with leaping flame. An enormous black wolf crouched between Cai and himself. Wisps of smoke and icy air drifted from its skin; its paws left frost marks on the glassy floor. Cold seemed to pour out of it, a numbing, aching cold, and its cunning eyes were blue shards of winter sky. The size of the creature amazed him, and he backed warily towards the stairs. But the Wolf had not noticed him; it was watching Cai. Already one of the torches on the wall was out and a mass of icicles hung from it; as Jamie watched, the Wolf swung its great head aside and growled a breath of icy air at another torch. It snapped out in an instant, the charred wood frozen to a glittering black lump.

Cai was taller, as if he had drawn himself up. With a snap of his fingers he relit the torch, and it scorched up with a great hiss of steam.

The Wolf's eyes went yellow in the light, and its jaws hung open so that Jamie could see its long blue tongue slavering over teeth sharp as icebergs. It slunk stealthily through the shadows.

'Come on,' Cai was muttering. 'I'm not going anywhere.' His yellow hair shone in the flames, and the very air around him seemed to crackle and shimmer. He had a long gleaming sword in his right hand, its edge smouldering red. Jamie wondered where it had come from.

Head low, the Wolf prowled on. Cai taunted it, his voice bitter with scorn. 'Come on, come and look at me, devil's lapdog! I'm Cai; have you heard of me? I'm the one who cut nine witches into shreds on Ystafinion! Do you think I'm worried about you?'

Ears flat, the Wolf snarled. Ice dripped from its teeth and froze on its jaws. Cai's figure flickered in the flames; he jerked forward, his voice low and mocking. 'Scared, little dog? Cai the Fair, Cai the Furious, slayer of monsters! Creep back to your dunghill while you still can!'

Like a shadow, the Wolf leapt.

Cai dropped. It landed and turned, but already his sword had flashed in a red arc, and as it struck the beast's flank the metal hissed and scorched; the Wolf roared with fury.

Jamie jerked back; the corridor was suddenly coated with ice and the breath on his lips had frozen. Eyes white, the Wolf snarled and slavered, twisted, struck out. Cai leapt, but the heavy paw slashed him; he gave a yell of rage and struck back, missed, and staggered out of reach. The torches died, and for a second both fighters were just shadows in a dim green crack; then the flames burned up like an inferno, roaring and licking the roof.

'Come on, hell-puppy!' Cai yelled, his face twisted

with anger. 'Palug's Cat would have eaten you for breakfast!'

Enraged, the Wolf flung itself silently through the darkness, and was on him before he could move, its teeth snapping and tearing at his throat, its icy breath frosting his face. Jamie gasped as they toppled and struggled; Cai cried out as the cold struck him. His sword arm was trapped; he waved the other and sparks lit the air; the Wolf yelped, twisted and bit at them, but still the man could not tug the sword free, and to his horror Jamie saw that ice was encasing them, a hard glass forming on their bodies and splintering as they struggled. The very air was aflame. Cai kicked and yelled with fury; the Wolf bit and tore at his arms and throat.

It was then Jamie moved.

He grabbed a torch from its bracket on the wall and ran forward, yelling and waving the flames. The creature jerked up its head and saw him. The eyes in the black mask narrowed; it growled and lurched at him, and he felt its shocking breath freeze the wood in his hand, numb him, coat his face and eyes with pain and hard white crystal. He dropped the torch and fell, half-blinded, on his hands and knees. The Wolf's breath was on his hair and its paws scrabbled at his neck, and as he beat it away, yelling, a vivid sword-flash burst out of the darkness, a sheet of flame that scorched the air as it passed. The Wolf screamed; its body writhed and collapsed on top of Jamie, knocking the breath right out of him; he smelt the cold, wet stench of its fur against his face. Something icy dripped down his neck. Then Cai heaved the heavy pelt off him, caught hold of his arm and pulled him up.

In a sudden echoing stillness the lamps were

burning blue. Then slowly the light steadied. For a long moment they gazed down at the black huddle.

Finally, Cai spoke. 'Stupid thing to do,' he said.

Jamie stared. 'You were in trouble!'

For a moment Cai's savage look swung on him; then the tall man shrugged. 'Trouble! I was just playing with it.'

'You ungrateful . . . boastful . . . unspeakable *idiot*,' Jamie spluttered. 'I wish it had killed you!'

'No you don't.' Cai grinned at him. 'Now come on. What we want is over here . . .'

Cai's arm was bleeding, Jamie noticed, and as he himself bent to gather up the Book the pain in his crushed ribs and shoulders made him wince. He was tired and aching and furious with Cai for his mockery.

'All that boasting,' he stormed. 'You were goading it on. It could have killed us both!'

'It didn't need encouragement for that.' Cai glanced at him narrowly. 'If a creature becomes angry enough it will become rash. Like you.'

Jamie shut up.

The prison door was made of a strange, hard crystal; Jamie had a shock when he realized it might be diamond. They turned the great key and heaved, both together, and even then they could only force the slab to a six-inch gap.

'Who's there?' asked a scared voice from inside.

Cai paused and grinned, wiping sweat from his face.

'Us!' Jamie said, relief shooting through him. 'Are you all right?'

'Yes!' Jennie's arm came round the door and touched him. 'A bit giddy. I just . . . was here. But get this thing open, will you!'

It took them a while, but finally the gap was wide enough even for Cai to squeeze through.

'What's going on? What was all that noise?' Jennie asked, taking in their bloodstained clothes and Cai's torn arm. But neither of them answered. They were staring at the boy who sat on the floor in the corner of the dirty cell: a boy a little older than Jennie, with hair the colour of corn and a smooth, serious face. He smiled up at them and moved a hand, and even that small movement clinked the gleaming glass chains that held him, wrist and ankle, to the wall.

'Cai,' he said, without any surprise. 'I was sure they would send you.' He frowned. 'I think I should warn you . . .'

'We know all about the Wolf.' Cai went forward quietly and knelt by the chains, tugging at the shining, slithering links.

'There's no lock,' Jennie said. 'I've looked.' She threw a worried glance at Jamie. 'What wolf?'

'Explain later.' He had been shaking his watch; the glass was smashed and he didn't know whether it was broken. About twenty seconds to go. Would it be enough? His heart sank at the thought of the long journey back.

Cai had the red sword in his hand; it seemed to come out of nowhere. He raised it and slashed at the chains, hard, with grim anger, and the glass shattered; shards flew out as he struck again, and one hit Jamie's cheek.

Painfully, Gweir stood up. He was thin; his hands were white as paper.

'Can you walk?' Cai asked, with stifled fury in his voice.

'I don't know.' The boy shuffled a few steps, rubbing his wrists. 'Yes. But not swiftly.'

'On my back.'

Hurriedly, Cai bent, and swung the boy up gently, then motioned Jennie in front of him. 'Go on! We may get out before they come. Hurry!'

They leapt the icy, sprawled carcase of the Wolf, its cold eye still staring upwards, and raced between the torches into the darkness, hurtling down the stairs, round and round at reckless speed, past the door where Jamie had hidden, down to the dark twist of the wall, and there was the Cauldron, huge and dusty on its platform in the empty hall. Jamie sped past it, but something reached out and grabbed him. As he stumbled, a foot shot out and Cai went sprawling over it, he and Gweir and Jennie a tangle on the floor. Cai groaned, and tried to struggle up, but a foot in his chest shoved him back.

'Lie still!' Gavan growled. 'Or I'll break your scrawny neck.'

15

The Wisdom of the Cauldron

The grip on Jamie's collar loosened; Morgant shoved him forward out of the shadows and looked at them all with a smile on his narrow face. He looked greyer here, and smaller, his beard glittering with crystals of frost. 'I see you found our lost friend,' he remarked. 'I must say, I hardly expected it. Very resourceful of you.'

'How did you get here?' Jennie snapped.

'Easily, my dear. Boat, the same as you. As for the unpleasant vulpine, our fierce friend here took care of that.'

Cai gasped as Gavan kicked his arm.

'Stop that,' Morgant said.

Gavan's head turned. 'Let me. Let me crush him. I'm sick of his insults and his arrogance. Let me finish him!'

'Just try,' Cai muttered through his teeth.

'I'm afraid we just haven't time for your delicate feelings, my friend.' Morgant came forward and took Gavan's elbow and pulled him back. 'Besides, we would hardly want the Emperor after our blood because of any damage to his precious foster brother, would we? No . . . the truth is, they don't matter any more. They've served their purpose. They can go.'

He bent down, smiling, and said it again, very

clearly, as if he was talking to infants. 'Do you hear? You can go.'

For a moment they were all too astonished to move. Then Gweir scrambled up, and Jennie helped Cai, who shook her off. 'What are you planning, old man?'

'My business. Yours is to take the boy and go home, quickly, before the ways are closed. Now's your chance. I won't stop you.'

For a second Cai hesitated. Then he caught Gweir's arm and started with him down the hall. 'If that's the way you want it.'

'No. *Wait!*'

Cai stopped. Everyone turned and stared at Jamie, who was clutching his rucksack in the shadow of the Cauldron. He planted his feet stubbornly and said it again. 'Wait! I'm not going – and neither should you. You know what they are going to do now. You know as well as I do!'

'I'll do as I like!' Cai snapped. 'We came for Gweir and we've got him. Unless we leave now, we'll *all* be prisoners!'

'He's right,' Morgant put in, nodding.

'I don't care!' Jamie swung to Cai. 'You know what the Cauldron is – you told me yourself. All knowledge in time and space. Are we going to leave that for them? For him! Imagine how he'd use it!'

'But Jamie,' Jennie put in, 'they can't steal it. Look at the size of the thing; it's enormous, and you know if you touch it . . .'

'I *know*, Jen! But they wouldn't have come this far without some plan.' He turned to Morgant, suddenly. 'You have, haven't you? You've come here for the Cauldron and you know exactly how to take it!'

For a moment even Morgant seemed taken aback. Then he shrugged. 'Perceptive, Jamie, as ever. Yes,

107

I am going to possess myself of the Cauldron.' He glanced around at their faces. 'My plans have been laid these many years, since only seven of the Emperor's Court limped home from the three ship-loads that set out. I realized then that force of arms was not the answer. The answer was magic, deep and dark. And so I searched. No one, not even Merlin, has searched as I did. I worked, and planned, and studied old books; I spoke with smiths and druids; I walked hour after hour under the stars, seeking the lore of hags and witches and anyone who might advise me. Oh, the Emperor would not have liked it, Cai, but I did it. Rune stones, ogham sticks – all the forbid-den things . . . I have consulted and connived with them all. And they gave me what all the Court of Logria could not. They told me how to steal the Caul-dron.'

Jamie was cold. 'Whoever is here just won't let you take it!'

'Ah yes.' Morgant spread his hands. 'And who is here?'

'You can't be such a fool,' Cai said, marching back, 'as to think this fortress is empty?'

In the dimness Morgant shook his head. 'Perhaps they are waiting to see what I will do. What about you? You will not stop me.'

'We're staying,' Jamie said.

Morgant's face was dark; there were hollows around his eyes. His hunger for the Cauldron shocked them. 'Are you now?' he whispered.

'Yes,' Jennie muttered.

Behind her, Cai glanced at Gweir. The boy shrug-ged his shoulders. 'A prisoner learns something of his captors,' he said quietly.

But Morgant did not hear him. He turned, waved

Gavan away from the Cauldron and stood before it, arms wide, his black, gleaming eyes fixed on the pearls and the dark-blue rim. Then he began to speak.

He began quietly, and slowly grew louder. The words were strange and foreign: a chain of harsh syllables, ugly words, not to be spoken. But Morgant chanted them firmly; and as his voice rose, it seemed to Jamie that the sky outside the windows grew darker, as if great clouds were rolling over the moon. Morgant's eyes were closed; the words poured out of him, ringing in the roof and walls with hissing, sibilant echoes. He spat them out of him like a snake.

The hall was black; sparks of light crackled around the Cauldron. As Jamie watched, it shivered and rippled, and still the words came, piling noise on noise, venom on venom, unbearable! His hands were over his ears, he was shouting and twisting to get rid of the shrieking, but it was inside him, building up to a terrible crescendo that burst in his head like a roar of pain.

He couldn't see but he leapt forward, grabbing at Morgant's tensed shape, dragging him down, away, anything to stop the unbearable syllables ringing in his head. Somewhere Cai was shouting, flames were flashing, but still Jamie hung on as the old man twisted and struggled and shoved him away. Jennie came from nowhere, but she too went sprawling, and Morgant staggered up, hands clenched, the muscles in his neck and face taut with triumph. In the spasm of the last words, he writhed, and reached out, and gripped the Cauldron.

And he did not vanish!

For a split second Jamie could not move; none of them moved. Morgant tightened his grip on the cold

109

blue metal and laughed. He began the words again, and Jamie was filled with despair; but even as he started, Morgant faltered and stopped. His smile faded. He twisted, moved this way and that, tried to pull his hands away; his face became a mask of unbelief and cold fear.

'He's caught!' Jennie whispered. 'He can't pull free of it!'

Gweir chuckled, in the shadows. Jamie turned and saw Cai's grin, saw Gavan lying flat on his back, beating off the globe of fire that flamed perilously over his eyes.

'Lie still,' Cai muttered, 'or I'll break your brawny neck!'

Morgant still twisted and pulled, panic in his face. 'Let me go!' he hissed furiously, but the Cauldron only caught his words and hummed them round and round the metal hollow in a murmur of despair.

And at once the hall was full of light.

It came from everywhere, in through the glass walls, making them pure gleaming slabs of crystal, making Jamie feel suddenly small, and grubby, and exposed. Into each of the nine mirrors around the Cauldron stepped a woman, identical, with a wolf at her side, appearing from nowhere with breathtaking suddenness. They were all tall, black-haired; their clothes were green as glass, and though they were reflections, he realized with a shiver that they each moved in a different way. Four on each side; one behind the Cauldron, and it was she who spoke.

'This place is not without its Guardians, strangers.'

Morgant bowed his head in silent fury.

'We are Fintan,' the woman said, her voice clear and cold and young. 'We are the ninefold, the three times three who guard the Cauldron of the King of

Annwn. Some of you,' she added, glancing at Gweir, 'know us already.'

They all spoke, Jamie thought, but with one voice. Just one.

'You have trespassed here,' the woman went on. 'You have killed one of our beasts; you have released our Prisoner; you have sought to steal the Cauldron of the King.'

'No!' Cai shouted, coming forward. 'Not the last. If you have been watching all this, you know that.'

Their eyes turned on him, cold and appraising. 'Once before, Cai,' the woman said, 'you came here for that reason.'

'Not this time.' Cai pointed to Morgant. 'There's your thief. The rest of us, apart from this – ' he nudged Gavan with his foot – 'didn't want it. The boy tried to stop him. You saw, Fintan. Don't pretend the Guardians of Knowledge are ignorant.'

For a moment Jamie thought they would be angry, but they made no sign. After a pause the woman said, 'You are still hot-headed, my friend. We have seen everything that has happened here – everything – since you came to this place. We have seen who is guilty, even in their thoughts, Cai Wyn.'

Cai looked startled. Then he pulled a wry face and said nothing.

The eyes of the women turned to Jamie. 'Come forward,' they said quietly.

Reluctantly, he stepped towards the Cauldron, but not too near. He tried not to catch Morgant's eye.

'Because of your action in trying to stop this,' Fintan said softly, 'you will be allowed to go from here.'

'But what about the others? What about Gweir?'

She smiled. 'The Tower must have its Prisoner.'

'But why?'

'Perhaps you should ask your friend.'

Slowly, Jamie turned and looked at Gweir. 'What do they mean?'

The boy smiled an old smile and shook his head. 'All who seek the Cauldron seek its power.' He glanced sidelong at Cai. 'That was the reason we came, all that time ago. We came for knowledge. And my punishment was that they gave me what I had come for. They allowed me to know. All the sorrows of the worlds, Jamie; all the darknesses and evils and their results – I have seen all that, as well as all that is good. That is why you heard me keening in the darkness. Now I know that knowing is not enough. I have learned wisdom, at last. That is why the Tower must have its Prisoner. It must teach him to open his heart.'

He smiled at the nine women. 'I have learned, Guardians. Now release me.'

The nine identical faces looked out on him, proud and compassionate. 'You have learned,' they said. 'Now others must.'

Suddenly, as one, they leaned forward, the wolves snarling and uneasy. They breathed softly, and at once a fire was kindled beneath the Cauldron, a strange fire of blue flames that flickered around Morgant's ankles without hurting him.

'No!' he roared. 'Not me! Listen to me, Guardians. I have power! I'm cunning in magic! I will not be imprisoned!'

'You were wrong twice,' the voices chanted. 'Neither force of arms, no, nor sorcery, will gain you wisdom. But suffering may.'

Smoke rose from the Cauldron; whatever was in it boiled and bubbled. Points of light glimmered in its depths; faint flickers of colour and shape moved in the scented smoke.

'Jamie!' Morgant writhed and struggled. 'Help me! Don't leave us here to rot!'

Jamie squirmed. 'Does he have to . . . ?' he began.

Fintan smiled. 'Yes. His heart is closed and black; both of their hearts. It is time they learned, Jamie.'

The smoke grew thicker. Morgant swore and cursed in fury; Gavan rolled himself up and held his head. Cai pulled them back as the wolves howled and snarled in the dimness. Then, slowly, the smoke cleared. Morgant was gone. Gavan was gone. The mirrors were empty.

Seconds later, the fortress had gone too.

16

Return to Logria

Fintan's Tower just winked out of existence.

It left them standing on a glassy outcrop in the lake, in a bitter wind that swept over the water, ruffling their coats and sleeves, and snatching their breath. In front of them the sun was rising, an unsteady red globe, flushing their faces. They stood in shock for half a second, then Jamie looked at his watch. The hands had not moved.

'It *has* stopped,' he whispered. 'Jen, we'll never get back!'

For a moment he had a vision of wandering for centuries in that desolate winter landscape; then Cai tugged him out of it.

'The boat! Quick!'

At least that was still there, drifting and bumping against the glassy rock. They grabbed it and climbed in. Jennie pushed off and the boat turned itself, moving out over the water.

Jamie broke the silence. 'What happens now?' he demanded.

Cai shook his head gloomily. 'It will take us a day, at least, to get back to the wood. Far too long. Resign yourself, Jamie.'

'Poor Morgant,' Jennie said suddenly, gazing back at the glassy green knoll.

'He deserved it.'

'Yes, but still . . .'

Cai shrugged. 'Don't worry about him. Worry about us.'

'He will be all right.' Gweir smiled at her. 'I promise you.'

The boat forged on, its prow whitening the waves. Spume and spray made rainbows over them and soaked them. Gweir trailed his hands in the water, his face to the wind as if he could never have enough of it. Cai tugged his dark coat round him, easing his stiff arm.

Slowly, the sun rose and the sky lightened. A flock of swans flew in from the south, circling low over the waves. Jamie stared at them. 'Look! Birds! Those are the first we've seen.'

He did not notice Gweir's private smile.

The swans splashed down into the water with a great rush of wings. Fish leapt out from under them, and suddenly, on the shoreline, the bird-song began. From tree to tree it sprang, and from further back, from the woods and valleys and grassy plains, a million whistles and warbles and sharp, piping notes.

Astonished, Jennie stood up in the boat. 'Look at it!' she muttered. 'It's all coming to life!'

In the warm glow of the sun, the lake and the sky were scattered with birds. Each tree on the lakeside was full of their movement, and among the reeds flocks of waterfowl fed and swam. Dragonflies dipped over the surface; squirrels climbed in the branches; wasps and bees crawled and hummed on the open lips of flowers. Almost as they watched, the trees were unfurling their leaves; the green web spread itself so rapidly that already the valleys in the furthest distance were emerald coverts in a yellow sweep of cornfields.

'What's happening?' Jamie yelled. He already had the Book open; spray splashed on to the page and he

wiped it off with his hand. The Book shot tendrils
and sprigs of greenery across its margins; drew quaint
flowers and strange double-headed birds brilliant in
blue and gold and red. Starting with a huge illumi-
nated letter, it wrote:

The Prisoner is released!

Despite his worries, Jamie laughed. 'Fine! And
what about us?'

The coloured inks ran riot across the page.

Fear not! See who awaits you!

The boat hit the shore with a bump, and Jamie
looked up.

On the edge of the bank above them, Hu Gadarn
stood, birds on his shoulders, a grin on his face, his
rusty clothes as green as the leaves, as if he, like all
the Land of Summer, had felt the change and the
magic of release.

'Good!' he roared, and the birds flew up from him
in a storm of feathers. 'Up you come! Quickly!'

Jennie was hauled up on to the bank; the others
scrambled after her. Cai pulled an apple from a tree
and tossed it to her. She bit it and giggled as the juice
ran down her chin.

'No time to waste,' the small man said. 'The way is
closing.'

'But it's too far!'

Hu laughed. 'Nowhere is too far. But first, Jamie,
I'm afraid you have something of mine.'

He had been expecting it, but that didn't make the
shock any easier. Reluctantly, he gazed down at the
Book, its cover smooth and black, the small glass

116

landscape set in its centre. And there they all were, five tiny figures by a blue enamel lake, and he could even just make out a miniature Book in one of their hands. With a rueful smile he opened the pages.

'I suppose I have to say goodbye.'

Goodbye, James Michael Meyrick. The spiky letters unrolled swiftly.

'You know, you could keep the Cauldron.' Jamie looked up. 'I'd settle for this any day if I could.'

Hu smiled.

'Oh, I know,' Jamie went on hurriedly. 'I know I can't, I know it has to go on, that someone else will need it. But . . . I suppose I've just got fond of it. It's as if there's a person in there . . . almost. Do you know what I mean?'

'Yes,' the small man said. 'I know.'

Jamie turned back to the Book. 'Thanks for helping us.'

The pleasure was all mine. This is for you.

A page detached itself and slithered out into his hand. It was blank.

I remember my friends, the Book wrote. *If you are ever in need, ask what you will and I will answer. But only once! Whatever is written will always be written. It may be in ten years or in fifty. I will reply. Good luck, Jamie.*

Slowly, Jamie closed the covers and handed the Book over to Hu, then folded the stiff page and put it in his inside pocket. It crackled there, reassuringly.

Hu looked at Cai. 'You will go with them?'

Cai shrugged. 'As far as I can.'

'Good. My best regards to the Emperor.' He held

out his hands. 'Farewell, Jamie, Jennie, Gweir, son of Summer. Remember Hu Gadarn.'

As he stepped back, the light faded; the landscape dimmed. Shivers of mist passed in front of them, as if for a moment the world was blotted out. Hu's shape darkened, grew, became hard; when Jamie put his hand out he felt rock, and he gripped it in a sudden giddiness of swirling patterns under his eyelids.

When he looked up again the sky was dark blue; the sun a black orb with a corona of fire. A high wind flattened his hair; the stone under his fingertips stood as tall as a man.

Jennie caught his elbow. 'The eclipse!' she murmured.

And as they watched from the hilltop, the sun's edge burst from its prison with a sliver of gold and flame that shot pain into their eyes, and they jerked their gaze away to the dim landscape and the black umbra hurtling silently away over the fields and the far hills.

A dog barked; birds sang as if it was morning. Steadily, the sun opened its eye. The astronomers straightened, applauded, slapped each other on the back; the rocks rang with their voices and the sound of the fiddle. Sunlight glinted on Cai's hair. They stood silent in the eruption of noise; no one even noticed them.

'Two minutes,' Jennie marvelled, finally. 'That's all it took.'

'It was really two days,' Jamie said.

'Neither.' Gweir gazed out at the hills, misty with coming rain. 'It was an eternity.'

Cai laughed. 'All wrong. It was just the twinkling of an eye.'

Jennie looked at him. 'And where is this Court of yours? How do you get home?'

'I am home.' He grinned at her look of confusion and thrust his hands in his pockets. 'First, little vixen . . .'

'Oh, stop that!'

'. . . First, we walk with you back to Caston. From there . . . Well, let's just say it's not far. Logria never is. Under the leaves, in the reflections of a pond, you might just see it.' He waved his hand vaguely at the winter country below them, at the farms and woods and the traffic on a distant road. 'Logria is out there.'

Jennie stared at it, and shrugged. 'If you say so.'

Over her head, Cai grinned at Gweir and Jamie. 'Come on,' he said. 'Before it rains.'

Author's Note

Some readers may be interested to know that many elements in this story are very old indeed. There are in existence fragments of a poem which date back to a thousand years ago or more, and which seem to tell of an expedition made by Arthur's men to steal a magic Cauldron from the Otherworld. The poem is known as 'The Spoils of Annwn' ('Preiddeu Annwn') and I have quoted it in the text. There are other stories too, of Arthur stealing a cauldron and releasing a prisoner. I have brewed up all these ideas and tried to make a new story from them.

Cai, of course, is the Sir Kay of the later 'King Arthur' stories, but in those his character sinks to being a bully and a fool. In the really old tales he is a hero and a wizard, and so I have made him.

And no, I don't know what Palug's Cat was, and I don't suppose by now anyone else does either!